Lady Moon

BY RACHEL STARR THOMSON

Lady Moon

Published by Little Dozen Press
Stevensville, Ontario, Canada
www.littledozen.com

Cover design by Mercy Hope
Copyright 2015

ISBN: 978-1-927658-41-3

Lady Moon

BY RACHEL STARR THOMSON

Little
DOZEN
press

Chapter 1

CELINE LANGUISHED SIX AND THIRTY DAYS in a cavern on the moon, where her uncle had unceremoniously tossed her. She had been in the habit of throwing her scrub brushes at his head whenever he poked it through the door of the Great Hall, and the last time she'd done it, he'd taken a fit of temper and had her sent—through whatever nefarious means he had at hand—to a place of such height, such distance, and such golden-white loneliness that no scrub brush could ever descend from its bitter reaches, hurled by ever such a temper.

She was still languishing with all her might and main when a wild head popped out of a smallish hole in the ceiling of the cavern. "Do me a good turn," it said with a friendly smile. "Marry me?"

Instinctively she looked for a scrub brush to pitch in the

head's direction, but as nothing came to hand, she listened to it. It seemed determined to talk.

"It would get us out of here," the head told her. "You and I, as husband and wife. I say, what are you looking for?"

"Something heavy," she answered.

"What for?" it asked.

"To pitch it at you," she answered.

"You'd miss," the head said cheerily. "Now don't look angry. You want something, I can see it in your eyes."

"I do," said she. "An older brother. Or," growing reflective, "a dog. You deserve to have *something* set on you." Her slender fingers ached for the lack of anything to throw.

A sudden racket of moving pebbles and shifting limbs was accompanied by a cloud of dust from above. The head was attached to a man—she had suspected so all along—and it proved as much by dropping through the hole, followed by the other necessary parts, into the cavern where she had up until now thought herself alone.

He was tall and thin, much longer than he was wide, and almost too long for most of his clothing. His hair was yellow and shocked about his head like a dandelion. His face was dirty but honest, cheerful, and undeniably friendly. He looked like the sort of young man who would duck if you threw something at him, but go on talking to you anyway—the sort who would eat whatever you set before him with a hearty good will, even if you had just refused to marry him.

He pulled a pair of rings out of his pocket. He held the larger one up. It was white gold, and it glinted in the pale light that shone within the cavern—a lonely light, as lonely in its ring-reflection as in its source. The moon shone everywhere, but it was a light you couldn't reach. You always felt as though you were standing outside a house, peering through drawn curtains at the light beyond that would never welcome you in.

"It is enchanted," he said. "It can take the wearer anywhere he wishes to go, but can take him back again only if it is accompanied by its double, fitted to the finger of a wife. An old magician gave it to me."

"And you used it to come *here?*" Celine asked.

"I did, in fact," he said. His eyes twinkled. There was a sort of light in them, too, but his was all open and flickering cheerfully in windows without curtains, saying "Come in, come in and stay a while."

She looked at him dubiously. "Not terribly clever of you, was it?" she asked.

"Perhaps not," he said. "But I've always wanted to see the moon." He looked up at the pale cavern ceiling. The hole he'd made in the roof opened all the way to the sky. Stars shone distantly down, their light made meager by the moon's native glow.

Celine pressed in. "But didn't you think your chances of finding a wife would be better elsewhere?" she asked.

He smiled. "I confess I didn't think much about it," he told her. "I supposed things would arrange themselves. And they have, haven't they? I've been watching you thirty-six days now, and I like you."

She cocked one finely drawn eyebrow. "It took you a month to decide that?"

"No, no," he said. "I liked you in the first week. But you were languishing so beautifully, I hated to interrupt."

She humphed a little and raised her lovely nose—it was lovely, to match the rest of her—pulled her cloak, grown ragged from a month's hard languishing, closer about her, and stuck out her hand. He dropped the smaller ring into it. She examined it in the cold light, holding it up to look through it. Something filmy shimmered across the center, pink and green and gossamer like the skin of a soap bubble. But when she squinted to be sure it was there, it dulled into cavern air.

"Hmmm," she said, still cocking her head and squinting through the ring. "Hum. Just how smart are these things?"

The young man smiled, as he had hardly ceased to do since dropping himself through the ceiling. "I beg your pardon?"

"How smart are the rings?" she repeated. "That is, if a young woman of suitable age and eligibility should put this on and go with you, would the rings know it if she was not precisely married to you?"

His face fell a little, dampening the fire in his eyes ever so slightly. "I couldn't say," he said. "They are *wedding* rings."

"But must they be exceedingly clever ones?" she asked.

He fingered his own ring. "Perhaps not," he said. "But do you mean that you won't marry me? I had hoped you would."

He looked so crestfallen, and the fire in his eyes was still so welcoming despite his hurt, that she felt sorry for him. She nearly reached out to touch him, but caught herself in time and drew her cloak tighter.

"I don't know you," she explained. She handed the ring back to him, not so coldly as she had taken it. "You may have been watching me for a month and six days, but I have never seen you before a few minutes ago."

Hers had in fact been a cold and lonely languishment. Some of that came back to her now, and she shivered.

"Of course," he said. Up jumped the welcoming candle in his eyes. All of a sudden he seemed a friend, and Celine was glad to have him there.

"Who are you?" she asked.

His eyes twinkled. "My name is Tomas."

"Celine," she said.

"O Lady Moon," he said, smiling. "You're not averse to fooling the rings, then? I wanted to see the moon, and I'm glad I came. But I have been here a very long time, and I feel impatient to go somewhere . . . larger. And warmer."

He was holding the ring out to her. The center of it was shimmering rainbow colours. She reached out, took it, spoke as she slipped it on. "How long have you been here?"

"I think," he said as he followed suit, and all around them the pale cold light started to blur together and then go dark and rushing like a fog-wind, "it will be ninety-three years next Tuesday."

And then she gasped. Her feet were touching the ground. The sun was beating down on her head with October caprice: deliciously hot, but apt to be lost behind cloud and cold wind at any moment. In the distance a forest was blazing in still life, inferno in the leaves.

Much closer, not twenty feet away, the remains of a house were smoldering. Tomas gave a little strangled cry and ran toward it. A sound came out of the smoke and ash—a meow. A pile of ashes shifted aside, and an animal, a cat that looked first grey and then orange, emerged from it. Against every law of fire and life, it was unharmed. It shook itself slightly, flicking a last bit of ash from its coat. The creature headed straight for Tomas, and he took it up in his arms. It turned its face out and stared at Celine with eyes that smoldered red and grey.

Celine stepped forward, shivering despite the heat of the sun and the cloak still drawn tightly around her. She was unsteady on her feet. The weird, rushing journey-that-had-not-been-a-journey still rattled around in her blood. She looked more closely at the blackened ruins. Here and there little fires still burned—on small corners of the floor, flaring up in places where nothing but ash could feed it. The fires should not burn, she knew that. Ash was not fuel; fire couldn't eat it. If anything, a fire so voracious should have eaten that cat. The house had been small, barely more than a single room, and from the bits of straw that collected in her hair, drifting on a smoky breeze, it had been thatched.

Tomas seemed to read her mind. "I thatched it myself," he said. There were tears in his blue eyes. "Thatched it and spelled it to keep it whole. It shouldn't have burned."

Celine shook her head. "It was no ordinary fire," she said. "I know who set it."

A single tongue of flame shot up from the ash very near her feet. She looked at it with strange calm. Tomas said something. Perhaps he was asking her who had done it. Whether or not that was his question, she answered it.

"It was my uncle," she said.

Tomas knelt down by the ash and started to pick through it with the end of a stick. Smoke rose everywhere he prodded. The ash was fine and silty; the stick ran smoothly through it. Nothing had survived. The cat stared into the smoke and yawned. Inside, its mouth was glowing amber. Its orange fur seemed to grey a little as wisps of smoke played around it.

"That isn't a cat, is it?" Celine asked. "It's a pyroline."

Tomas looked up with appreciation. "Good eyes. How did you know? Not many people have ever seen one." He reached out and stroked the cat, still balancing on his heels with the end of his stick smoking in the ash.

"My uncle likes fire," Celine said. "He had a few pyrolines around. Bigger ones."

They had not been friendly creatures. When Celine was a few years younger they had prowled the edges of the grounds at night and crept into her nightmares with their glowing eyes and smoking footsteps.

Tomas's eyes grew thoughtful. He stood slowly, looking down on the remains of the house. Celine felt suddenly sad for him. She gestured toward the pile of ashes, its few remaining pieces of framing sticking up like signposts in the smoke. "Was this your home?" she asked.

"One of them," he answered. He chewed his bottom lip thoughtfully. "Why here?" he asked.

The question hadn't been addressed to Celine. She stepped slowly around the perimeter of the ashes, close enough to touch the largest piece of framing, blackened and flaking away as it was. In the corner just below it, a fire flared up three feet, sizzling and crackling before it drew downward and began to lick along the edges where the house walls had been. The pyroline, now twining itself around Celine's ankles, hissed. Through her skirt, she could feel its body temperature rise.

Tomas frowned down at the unruly flame. "Enough of that," he said abruptly. He reached into his patchy cloak, pulled out a pinch of something powdery, and threw it down over the ashes. It crackled all the way through the air, and when it settled on the ash, a bright light flashed. Celine blinked away the spots in her eyes. The ruin was no longer smoking. It looked cold and dead and very old.

A cold wind was blowing. It pulled dark wisps of cloud like yarn overhead and knitted them together to darken the whole sky. A few drops of cold rain rode down from them. Celine gathered her cloak again, wishing it was thicker, as she'd wished every day since her uncle's banishment, and looked up at the unfriendly gloom. She had never loved nature—had never really known what to do with it—and though she was no longer on the moon she felt suddenly insecure. One misery was not an especially good trade for another.

"Lady Moon?" Tomas's voice pulled her gently from her thoughts. She looked down at him. He was standing in the very center of the ashes, holding out his hand as though to welcome her through a door.

The rain was coming down harder. The pyroline pushed against her ankles and stalked toward Tomas, its grizzled orange head down. She cocked her head without knowing she was doing so, walking slowly forward with a cynical expression she couldn't help. His hand was still held out, and with the long breeding of nobility that did after all run in her veins, she reached out and took it with the tips of her fingers. She ducked as she entered the patch of ash, though there was no door frame through which to duck, and a moment later stood beside Tomas in the grey.

No rain reached her there.

She looked up wonderingly. There was no roof overhead; no walls. The wide sky with its gathering storm and distant ridge of trees bending in the wind and suffering their leaves to be stripped were open to her eyes, but the wind could not be felt. In fact, the air around her felt close—warm—almost homey.

He smiled. At his feet, the pyroline grew a little, its fur thicker, its limbs and head bigger. Its eyes started to smolder, but only faintly. Tomas saw Celine's nervous glance.

"Never fear," he said. "The ashes are dead. He only grows because fire has been here, but he'll stay small."

Celine was about to say something in response, but Tomas walked past her in the small space and she was obliged to gather her cloak and skirt to keep him from stepping on the hems. He walked to the imaginary door through which Celine had ducked and raised his hands. As she watched, fascinated, he gathered the falling raindrops and began to spread them in the shape of a door frame. They hardened under his hands like dull crystal, and in a few minutes a door frame was plainly visible, murky white against the dark horizon. He looked back at her for a moment with a smile.

"I made it last time of mud bricks and clay," he said. "It was far nicer—far more a home. I didn't mean to bring you here, but as we've come, I am sorry there is so little to welcome you." As he talked he spread his hands along the invisible walls as though he was smoothing something down, and once again the raindrops hardened against his hands. This time they did not grow solid and white, but remained transparent, the storm outside still visible through a slight silver sheen. Lightning flashed, and the walls seemed, for an instant, to be filled with lightning themselves. Tomas frowned up at the missing roof.

"Thatch," he said. "The raindrops are all wrong. They won't shape properly for thatch."

Celine's legs were growing oddly weak beneath her, and she sank slowly down on the soft ash. "What are you building with?" she asked.

"Memory," he answered. "Memory and whatever I can find to fashion over it."

He reached up and fingered the clasp of his patched cloak, still frowning. The expression hardly seemed to belong on his face. His long fingers paused a moment, and then he whipped his cloak off, its patched material sweeping through the room so it nearly clipped the pyroline's ear. The creature yowled up at him and moved closer to Celine. She could feel the heat of its body.

Tomas picked carefully at one hem of his cloak until he had opened it up, and working quickly so that Celine could hardly follow his movements, he began to tear the fabric apart. Long threads, many of them thin and barren, separated from each other. Celine started as a raindrop landed on her face, and then another on her neck, trickling down just inside the neckline of her dress. It was cold on her skin like the moon distilled. She looked up. Clouds had entirely covered any sunlight that still remained. A few more raindrops reached her. Memory was growing too thin to hold them back alone.

"Can I help you?" Celine asked Tomas. She should have asked before, she realized. He was sitting in a heap in the ashes, arms and legs as tangled as the cloak threads, attempting to weave them together in a new, loose way that would cover most of the ceiling. There wasn't enough thread. They would be lucky if half the roof was covered, and that would be full of holes. Hardly thinking, Celine reached for the clasp of her own cloak.

Tomas saw her do it. He shot her such a look that she stopped at once and dropped her hand back down. She remembered a long time ago, when her parents were still alive, she had gone outside and played in the apple barrels. When she came back in she was full of dust, leaves, and bits of spiderweb, and her father had given her a look just like Tomas's. It was a look which said with utmost clarity, "Princesses don't *do* that." She had never played in the apple barrels again.

Tomas's odd network of threads was finished. He threw it up and smoothed it over the ceiling, where it hardened and held in place much as the raindrops had done, taking on a vague resemblance to thatch—albeit with odd threads of brown, purple, and red worked into its overall yellow.

Thunder crashed as Tomas leaned against the wall opposite Celine with a sigh and slid down to the floor. The ashes were unusually soft, almost cushy—taking the form, Celine realized suddenly, of something that had been here before, a rug or heap of blankets or even perhaps a bed. He smiled again. It was his native expression, she thought. He smiled the way her old golden dog had always smiled. It struck her as a cruel thought, but somehow, as she looked at him and smiled tentatively back, it wasn't.

She leaned against the raindrop wall behind her. It supported her. She expected it to be cold and hard, but the feeling against her back was one of gathering warmth and give, like a mud-and-clay wall that had collected the warmth of a hearth fire for several hours. The air felt even heavier and warmer than it had before the walls and half-ceiling, even though an occasional raindrop found its way in through the part of the ceiling that was patched only with memory. She bowed her head so that her cloak came up over her cheeks to shield herself from the drops. Tomas was already falling asleep. She thought for a minute that he was heating the house somehow, but then she realized, as a grey-orange form tucked itself up by her feet, that it was the pyroline's unusual body heat doing it. She was glad it was a small one. The one time she'd gotten too close to her uncle's pyrolines, the heat had left a burn mark on her hand.

Her eyelids began to close. She had not been warm in a month and a week. She hardly needed the cloak, but she kept it pulled tightly around her anyway, just to bask in the comfort of it. She didn't really think she ought to be sleeping. She didn't even really know where she was. *Princesses,* she thought to herself with an unconscious look on her face much like her father's, *don't sleep beneath memory-and-thread roofs with small pyrolines and strange men they don't even know.*

Her last waking breath came out as a sigh, and in it she remembered that Tomas had wanted to marry her.

Chapter 2

TOMAS WOKE FIRST. THE STORM HAD CLEARED during the night, and the rising sun came over the tree-rimmed ridge out of a bed of red-purple and orange. Around it the sky was blue, above it dark and still twinkling with a few hardy stars.

Celine had gone to sleep in the western corner, so the sun coming through the raindrop walls lit her up. It didn't wake her because she was tired, as only one who has languished long in a cold exile can be tired.

She was beautiful. Anyone with eyes could see that. Her hair was long and glossy and forest-brown; her eyes blue. She wore a dark blue dress that made her skin look pale, but moon-pale—apt to glow or turn to cream, but never to look sickly or weak. She was slender and graceful, with a very fine nose and a pair of eyebrows which could and regularly did express scorn, surprise, or question. Her hands were a princess's hands. Every bone, every vein was fine and beautiful. Yet they were worn, in contrast to their born nature, chapped and calloused.

This observation led Tomas to reflect on what he had learned of Celine since he'd first seen her on the moon. He hadn't seen her arrive, but he knew that only magic could send someone so far, and only an enemy would do such a thing—unless, of course, you were possessed of a pair of traveling rings and a desire to see the outreaches of the spheres. Celine evidently possessed neither.

Then there was her startling announcement that her uncle had lit the fire that burned down Tomas's house. He had ignored it.

He played with the ash as he watched her in the rising sunlight, making little circular paths through it. Ignored it, but not missed it. He'd understood her perfectly; understood her even to the extent of knowing exactly who her uncle was. He was Ignus Umbria, the only living man who knew how to set a Ravening Fire, collector of magical artifacts and dangerous creatures, and the wealthy lord of the Western Kingdom.

The circular paths Tomas's fingers traced caught his eye. He tipped his head, looking at them sideways, and smiled. That particular squiggle reminded him of a bird. He drew a beak and a pair of legs and ruffled feathers. A fat, round, ruffled bird. The sun was up higher. It was coming through the raindrop walls and making rainbows in the air. The pyroline rose from its place by Celine's face, stretched, and yawned. The amber of its mouth was pale, more like a flower than like a fire.

Celine went on sleeping. Ignus Umbria's niece, rescued out of exile, sleeping in his house. Tomas smiled at the thought, but it was a sad smile.

Of all the things he knew about Umbria, and there were many, foremost in his mind was that he, Tomas Solandis, had been born for the sole purpose of destroying him.

Celine sighed and stirred. A flock of birds outside landed on the roof and started pecking at the thatching, pulling out threads and causing dust—straw dust, called out of memory by Tomas's handiwork—to rain down almost on Celine's head. Tomas jumped up and hit the thatching several times so the birds would fly away. When he looked back down, Celine's eyes were open. The expressive face told him all he wanted to know. She was scrutinizing him.

"Why has my uncle burned your house down?" she asked.

Tomas started to answer, but he stopped himself. He wasn't entirely sure, after all. Other words popped into his mind, so he voiced them.

"Your uncle has skill," he said. "Skill but not much virtue."

She raised one exquisite eyebrow. "Do you know him?" she asked.

"I don't have to," Tomas answered. He dropped into a crouch, looking intently through the dusty air to her face. "Listen, are you sure you don't want to marry me?"

She regarded him a moment without a word. "I still have nothing to throw at you," she finally answered.

He smiled. "Do you always throw things at your admirers?"

"No," Celine answered. "Usually only at my uncle. I don't have admirers."

It was Tomas's turn to raise an eyebrow. "That," he told her frankly, "is impossible."

She humphed and rose, shaking out her cloak. Ash and thatching dust swirled down together from the folds. Like star-glitter around the moon.

The pyroline meowed. They both looked down at it. Its grey was growing darker, its orange fur deeper, less stable. Its eyes were starting to glow. Celine sniffed the air.

"Smoke," she said.

"Talent," Tomas said. He folded his arms and regarded the little hut with its water-walls and threaded ceiling over a floor of soft ash. "The fire will lick it all up again, I'm afraid."

Celine looked nervous. "We'd best be off then," she said. Her eye was on the pyroline, which was looking less like its tame self with every passing moment.

"Did you ever hit him?" Tomas asked.

She looked up. "Excuse me?"

"Your uncle," he said. "With the scrub brush. Did you ever hit him?"

She paused a moment, deliberating, and then answered, "Yes. Often."

"And he sent you to the moon because . . ."

"He didn't think I could throw that far," she said. She put her nose slightly in the air. "He didn't leave me anything to try it with."

"Do you love your uncle?" Tomas asked.

The eyebrows raised again. "I beg your pardon?"

"He is your family." They had not moved from the ashen floor. The smell of smoke was growing stronger. The pyroline had begun, not to purr, but to mewl with a high-pitched rumble that was entirely unique to fire-cats. Celine shifted her feet, eying the dull white door frame behind Tomas.

"After a fashion he is my family. He did send me to the moon. He doesn't love me, and I can't say I'm terribly sorry for that."

She hadn't answered his question at all, but Tomas nodded as though she had. An image of Ignus Umbria's face came to his mind, as he had seen it imprinted on gold coins. The face was long, thin and yet sagging slightly at the mouth. The brow was heavy and hung over piercing eyes. It was a face that would send children and small dogs running for cover.

He had a sudden mental image of the face being surprised by a bristled projectile hurled in its direction by the girl who now stood looking nervously at the walls of his hut, and he laughed out loud.

As he did, the edges of the dull white door frame turned brown, and tiny flames began licking around it. The pyroline let out a yowl.

Celine could take no more. "*Will* you get out of the way?" she burst out.

Tomas got out of the way. He stepped through the door frame, took Celine's hand, and half-pulled, half-escorted her through the rectangle of flame. The pryoline shot out the door in the next minute, its whole body smoking. The ends of its orange hairs were standing on end and wavering like candle flames. It streaked between Tomas's feet and stopped itself three feet away, licking its paws as it shrunk down to normal size with an expression that was meant to be dignified.

Celine looked as ruffled as the cat. She smoothed her dress out, her slender hands shaking slightly, as behind her the fire grew. A moment later the whole hut was up in flames, and pillars of smoke rose to the ridge. Tomas watched and shook his head.

"It was a good little home once," he said. "I lived in it fifty years. Pity it should go to fire." He faltered a little. "I'd hoped to watch it crumble into well-loved old dust one day."

Celine finished his thought for him, but not out loud. *And all you have is ashes.* That, she thought, was typical of her uncle. She remembered very well one day when she was a small girl. She had been playing in the courtyard with her skirts neatly arranged around her, dancing a little doll in the blue folds. It was a rag doll. One of the housekeepers had made it for her, and she loved it. And then her uncle—she never thought of him by his name, just as her mother had never referred to him by name but always called him "your uncle"—had charged out the western door in high excitement, his long face ruddy with glee as it always was when something particularly awful had happened.

"Child!" he had shouted, "I've done it!" And he'd snatched up her doll, whirled away on one heel, and rushed back through the western door with Celine on his heels. She had followed him, white-faced, with her hands clasped together in silent pleading that she might have her doll back. They had gone all the way up to the wide tower where her uncle had been so long in preparing things.

And he proved that he had done it. Had learned how to send things a very great distance. He had shown her by sending the doll to the other side of the world. She had watched gravely, congratulated him, gone back down to the courtyard alone, and cried.

Years later he'd hauled her back up to that tower and sent her even farther than the doll. She hadn't looked to see if that gleeful look was visible beneath the red mark and soapsuds on his high forehead. She hadn't really cared.

Tomas sighed. With the sigh, a look of determination came over his face. Celine saw it and wondered about it, but she did not ask. Tomas turned and began to stride toward the ridge.

"There is," he said, "or was, a village over the ridge. Past that are the Fallow Fields of Brusa, and beyond that the sea—and Meru, the city on the sea."

His voice carried to her in the wind that blew down the ridge into their faces. He didn't raise his voice or speak with any unusual force, but she could hear him as clearly as if she was walking right behind him and not—as she was—lagging. She waited for him to stop or turn or egg her on, but he did none of them. It was just as well. She had no intention of ceasing to lag, not if he threatened to throw her over his shoulder and carry her up the hill if she couldn't keep up.

The path headed up the ridge, and Celine's legs began to burn with the effort of climbing it. She looked up to the sky as she walked. It was clear and pale blue. Last night's storm had left not a trace of itself. A flock of birds, jabbering loudly, turned circles in the air ahead of them. They swooped in and skirted the edge of the trees before rising raucously higher, and then came down and did it all over again.

The wind coming over the ridge was cold, and it smelled like salt. It was a sea wind, blowing down from northern places. Celine watched Tomas's wild yellow hair stand straight up as the wind blew through it. His thin shirt beat against his arms and around his back like a flag straining to unfurl itself. She looked a little closer and saw the little holes all along the hems of the shirt's arms, and a large hole right in the middle of the back. Indignation rose suddenly within her. He must have been cold on the moon, with nothing but his threadbare clothes and the now-incinerated cloak to keep him warm. A bear in all its grand fur would have been cold on that moon. And while it was true that Tomas had sent himself there, for some reason Celine could not yet fathom, it still seemed unfair that he should have been there so poorly dressed. And now that his house should be in ashes. If she turned her head and looked down the ridge, she could still see the thickly rising smoke.

Tomas and Celine did not speak to each other as they went over the ridge. He was lost in thoughts of his own—thoughts of Ignus Umbria and exactly what it meant that his niece was trailing along behind him. Thoughts also of his other homes, and where he should go now that his hermit hut was gone.

Celine was mentally assessing every article of Tomas's wardrobe and growing more indignant by the minute. She was also making plans to go home.

Their thoughts collided minutes after they reached the village and settled themselves into chairs in a small tavern.

"How long would the journey home take, do you think?" she asked.

He looked at her in surprise. "Home? To Umbria's palace?"

"It is my palace," Celine informed him. "My uncle and I have equal rights."

"He sent you to the moon," Tomas reminded her.

"I'll keep out of his way," she said. She reached out and flipped the edge of Tomas's sleeve. "Your clothes are disgraceful. How the wind doesn't tear you to shreds I can't imagine."

If the sudden change in topic bewildered him, he didn't show it. "I'd rather you didn't go back to the palace," he said.

"It's not like there's much of an option," Celine said. She stood and walked around the table, coming to a stop just behind Tomas's shoulder, where a particularly large hole was tearing itself in the stitching. She snapped her fingers at a barmaid who was passing through. The girl gave her a blank look.

"Needle and thread, if you please," Celine said.

Tomas started to twist himself around, but Celine's hand on his shoulder stopped him. "Hold still," she said.

"You don't need to stitch me up," he said.

"You look like a scarecrow," she said. "I have some pride, if you don't." The barmaid reappeared with needle and thread. Celine took it, balanced herself against a chair, and started sewing the shirt. Her needle barely missed Tomas's skin, and he watched with his head twisted to one side and his yellow eyebrows set slightly higher than usual.

"Anyway," Celine muttered, "it's cold. Holes in your clothes don't do much good."

He smiled. "Can you cobble shoes?"

She glanced down at his boots. She'd noticed them, of course—the soles coming off with every step he took, the hole in one toe where one atrocious grey knitted sock stuck out, losing bits of yarn to the stones and thorns of the pathway. "No," she said.

She bent a little closer to his shoulder. The needle darted in and out. She pricked her own finger and yelped. She'd no sooner stuck the offended digit in her mouth than the door of the tavern burst open and a man barreled forth, leaving a group of others to gawk, and cast himself at Tomas's feet.

"Sun-God!" he exclaimed. "You've come back!"

Tomas sighed. Celine backed away, eyeing the men in the door warily as she sucked on her finger and kept her feet well away from the little man who was now groveling in uncomfortable proximity to her own skirts.

"Look," Tomas said, laying his golden hand on the man's shoulder. "I've been over this."

The man was still bowing, his nose near the floorboards, but he shook his head emphatically. "Welcome, welcome, Sun-God."

Another man stepped out of the group. He was tall, strong, sharp-eyed. His voice was smooth and disconcerting.

"Welcome, Moon-Goddess," he said.

Celine opened her mouth to protest, dropping the hurt finger, but the words were interrupted before she could get them out. The men had fanned in from the doorway and were slowly moving to every side. She turned completely around to look behind her. Another man stared coldly back.

They were surrounded.

Chapter 3

THE MAN AT TOMAS'S FEET WAS VERY OLD. It surprised Celine to realize it. He had moved so quickly and cast himself to the ground with such abandon that she'd imagined him to be young enough to bounce. In reality, the thin hair on the man's head was white, his eyes watery, his skin wrinkled. He looked up at Tomas's distressed face with tears of joy.

The younger man who had addressed Celine as moon-goddess was another story entirely. He was strong and impressive. He wanted her to look at him: to meet his eyes and come under their power. She knew it, and so was determined not to do so. Instead she knelt beside the old man and took his arm gently.

"Come, grandfather," she said. "On your feet."

Tomas nodded, taking the old man's hands and helping him stand. "Yes," he said. "Please. None of this kneeling."

"You came back!" the old man said, his eyes still full of tears. "I told them you would. The day you left, I turned and I told them all, and none of them believed me."

Tomas looked surprised. "You were there?" he asked.

The old man nodded. "Ninety-three years ago. I was only a little boy. But I've believed; I've always believed."

He leaned a little on Celine as he stood. He was unsteady on his feet and heavier than he looked. Tomas reached out and laid his hands on the man's shoulders, and then he kissed him on each cheek.

"Bless you," Tomas said. "You're truly faithful. But I am no god."

"Come now," said a loud voice—the other man, the leader whose self-important voice Celine had decided she detested. "You have been gone for ninety-three years without aging a day. You come and go in a flash of light. You build huts that do not fall."

Tomas looked affronted. "Did you try to knock it down?"

The man folded his arms and spread his feet out a little farther apart. "This old man said it was built with a god's hands. I wanted to prove you before I would worship."

Tomas turned a funny shade of red. "Destruction isn't proof of anything but your own foolishness."

"It stood," the man said.

"It's in ashes now," Tomas answered. "Explain that, if you're so bent on worshiping me."

The old man, still leaning on Celine, was beginning to tremble. His innocent face was pained, confusion in his eyes. "My lord," he said, speaking this time to the village leader, "this is not how we should welcome the long-lost Sun-King."

A change came over the leader's bearded face. "Of course not," he said. "Forgive me." He stepped forward and took Tomas by the arm, like one friend confiding in another. With a look at Celine and the old man that demanded they follow, he pulled Tomas out the door and into the village street.

"There is a church," he said. "A shrine, if you will, just at the end of this street. Come with me, please. It's the proper place to welcome you."

He hustled them down the street to a tall square building, with high crystal windows that let the sun pour in near the top. He opened the door, ushered Tomas in, and took Celine's arm, practically thrusting the old man aside. The next thing Celine knew, she was inside the square tower beside Tomas, with the bearded man facing them both. The old man had been left outside, the door slammed in his face.

"Look here," the bearded man said. "I've built you a good thing. You can't be fools enough to step in and ruin it."

"I don't know what you've done," Tomas said. He was looking around and up the wooden sides of the tower at the sun pouring in through the windows. "This is the place where I put the ring on and disappeared."

"Ninety-three years ago?" the bearded man said. "I confess I didn't think you would come back. I don't know what you are, but you're not human."

"Not entirely, no," Tomas confessed. "Well, not as you would define human."

"That's irrelevant," the man said. "What matters is that I've spent most of my life playing on this village's fear of you, and I won't let you waste it all."

Indignation boiled up inside Celine. "That old man didn't seem afraid of him," she said.

"Him? No, he's a fool. He loves you. Won't take a hint—hardly hears a word I say. But he saw you disappear in a burst of light, and he saw you do miracles—he says—when he was a boy. He's invaluable. Eyewitness testimony to give weight to everything I tell the others."

Tomas drew himself up. "You are a villain," he said.

"Of course," the bearded man answered. "My name is Malic. This is my town. I'm the wealthiest man from here to Meru, and I tell you, if you'll help me, I'll give you a piece of it. All you need do is play along for a few days—you and your lady friend. Then you can be on your way, none the worse for it."

"And that old man?" Tomas asked. "Will he be the worse for it?"

"He's seen you now," Malic said. "It's what he's been waiting for his whole life. If luck has it, he'll die now that he's done it."

Celine nearly boiled over. "You heartless . . ." she sputtered. The man was paying no attention to her. His eyes were on Tomas.

"So," he said. "Consider it carefully."

"I have considered it," Tomas said. "I consider that this must stop. All of it. Now."

Malic's face grew dark with anger. He reached out and grabbed Celine's arm, pulling her toward him. "I don't think you want to oppose me," he said.

In the next moment he shouted with pain and dropped Celine as if she were a snake. She was flushed and breathing hard; her head high in outrage. Malic pulled her sewing needle out of the back of his hand. He lifted his other hand as though he would strike her, but Tomas intervened. With one swift movement he crossed the floor, pinned both of Malic's strong arms to his side, and lifted him high off the ground.

The sun shining through the windows came down on Tomas as he stood like a stalk of corn holding a bull. It lit up his bright hair and glowed in his long, lanky limbs. Malic turned first red with anger, then pale beneath his brown beard as he realized he could not free himself. Tomas showed no sign of strain, nor of any need or desire to put Malic down. He looked as though he could hold the bull up forever.

"Put me down this instant," Malic said through his teeth. "Now!" He was still pale.

"Celine," Tomas said. "Open the door."

"Gladly," she answered. She opened the door and swept

through it into the street. The group that had followed Ma-lic and the old man to the tavern had gathered others, and the street was now full of gawking onlookers. Just up the street, stocks waited with a town crier's bell above them. Celine marched up to the bell and began ringing it with all her might. Tomas followed, still holding Malic as high as his lanky arms would stretch.

More people spilled into the streets. They gawked at the sight of their discomfited priest and ruler. Tomas carried him up the street and stopped beneath the stile where Celine stood, still ringing the bell. She stopped and let the sound die down. Tomas looked calmly out at the crowd.

"This man," he said, "is a bully and a liar."

Amid the murmurs of the crowd, Celine jumped down and opened the stocks. Tomas plunked Malic into them, and Celine pushed them closed, stepping on top of them for good measure. Malic glared up at her with all the hatred he could muster. Even that fell a little flat. It was difficult to hate thoroughly in such embarrassing circumstances.

"But," one of the women in the crowd began, "Sun-God . . ."

Tomas cut her off by shaking his head so vigorously that flashes of sunlight seemed to fling away from his shining head. "No more of that nonsense," he said. "There's no god about me. Next person who says there is will hear it from me." He thumped the stocks. "*This* is what comes of ascribing deity to a man. Bullying and lies. This, now, this is a man who's tried to take advantage of all of you, and I hope you'll shake yourselves free of him. Entirely free. Do you understand me?"

The crowd nodded and murmured in assent. Malic appeared to be choking back some retort. Celine's feet were in close proximity to his face, and he eyed the heels of her boots with apprehension.

"Good," Tomas said. "Off with you then. Go on—go home, go back to work. There's nothing more to see here."

He turned his back on the crowd suddenly, crouching down in front of Malic.

"Now listen, you," he said. "I may not be a god, but I'm not a pawn either. If you mistreat these people in my name again I'll have something to say to you about it, and you'll wish yourself back in the stocks."

Malic spat at Tomas's boots. He cast a quick glance over at Celine, but Tomas was in the way—she couldn't kick him. "You've ruined everything," Malic said.

"That's right," Tomas said. "For good and ever."

He stood and dusted off his knees, though his entire outfit was so dusty that it hardly made any difference. He smiled at Celine.

"Well done," he said.

"Thank you," she answered.

They turned together and saw him at the same time.

The old man was still standing in the street. Everyone else was in the process of going, but he stood looking at them without moving. Tears were running down his aged face.

Celine felt suddenly as though her heart was wringing its hands. She went to the old man and took his arm gently. "What's your name, grandfather?" she asked.

"Monk," he said tremulously. The name barely made it past his lips. He was shaking with utter misery.

"Where do you live?" Tomas asked.

Monk raised a shaking finger and pointed at the stocks. "With him," he answered.

Tomas clicked his tongue. "That won't do. You have nowhere else to go?"

The old man shook his head. He started to turn away. Malic's words came back both to Tomas and Celine—*"If luck has it he'll die now that he's seen you."*

Celine raised her eyes to Tomas's face. It was her intention to do something—say something—to make Tomas help. She would beg him on bended knee to take the man along with them, if there was nothing else to be done. But she stopped as soon as she saw his face. He didn't need begging. That old welcoming candle was still flickering in his eyes, but this time it looked as though it would envelop the old man in its flame.

Tomas darted around the old man so that he stood before him again. "Come with us, Grandfather Monk," he said. "I've a roof and a bed and a pot of stew waiting. There's enough to go around."

Something strange kindled in the old man's eyes. Something like hope—like a very old dream coming to life. For an instant he looked like a little boy who wanted nothing more than to follow his idol to the moon. But the instant passed, and he looked like an old man again.

"I can hardly walk from one street to the next," he said. "I would slow you far too much."

He shook his white, white head, and turned away. He started to shuffle down the street. He was right, of course. He looked as though he might topple over at any moment.

But he didn't. Tomas danced into his path again, and with a bow of his head and a twinkle of his eyes, he picked the old man up like a baby in his arms, holding the white head against his heart. He looked at Celine with bright eyes. "We'll be off then," he said. "To Meru."

Chapter 4

THE OLD MAN LOOKED FRIGHTENED for the first few minutes that Tomas carried him. Then he relaxed like a child relaxes against his father, and took in the world through his watery eyes as they walked. Tomas looked like a boy carrying a feather, so little did he stagger under the old man's weight. Celine walked at his elbow, keeping an eye on Grandfather Monk and casting disapproving glances at the holes in Tomas's shirt. She was not sorry to have stabbed Malic with the needle—he had fully deserved it—but she rather resented him for not giving it back.

They walked over the Fallow Fields of Brusa: acre upon acre of smooth, rolling land, still rutted in places from the marks of old ploughs and wagons, still growing wild patches of wheat and oats amidst the grass. Celine had seen the fields before from her uncle's telescope—one of his proudest possessions, able to look through both space and time. She had looked on the fields in the days when Brusa was still inhabited, when happy children ran behind strong sowers, playing with geese and gulls in the sun. She had tried to see the day when they disappeared, but it was no use. No one knew why the fields of Brusa lay fallow. No one knew what had happened to take or drive its people away. Even her old tutor, an expert in history and covert borrower of her uncle's telescope, had never managed to zero in on the mystery. Her uncle had discovered the man's borrowing and thrown him out of the palace shortly before he demoted Celine from education to floor-scrubbing.

It took days to make it through the fields. Grandfather Monk wavered between exhaustion and sickliness and a sort of perky curiosity that seemed to give him strength. When he was thus awake he would hold his head up, peeking over Tomas's arms and taking everything in. Once or twice he even asked to walk.

"Please," he said, beaming shyly at Celine once Tomas had set him down, "would you allow me to escort you?"

She took his arm and discovered to her satisfaction that he was the perfect gentleman, even if he did lean a little heavily. He pointed out everything of interest and complimented her whenever the occasion arose. He was a simple man, without many mental faculties, and Celine wondered if he had always been that way or whether time had taken its toll. Either way he was good company. She warmed to him more with every step.

For supper on the first night, Tomas set Grandfather

Monk down and went roaming in the fields. He came back with grains of wheat and oats, which he somehow managed to cook into a sort of porridge. It was tasty and satisfying. On the second night, Celine took a handmade bow and arrows and marched into the fields alone. She shot three birds and brought them back to roast over a fire. Tomas thanked her with great appreciation.

"You have talent, Lady Moon," he said.

On the third night, they reached Meru. They crested a hill and there it was: shining in the darkness below them, lights reflected on the sea that stretched out into blackness on the other side. Waves beat against the shoreline and rocked the boats that lay at anchor. Laughter and music drifted through the dark. Across from them, nearly level with the top of the hill, was a high clock tower looking out over the bay. Its round face was lit like a moon itself.

Tomas smiled at the sight of it. "Home," he said to Celine. Grandfather Monk was asleep in his arms. He hefted him a little closer and started down the steep path to the city.

The streets were close and damp. The air from the sea was cold. Celine drew her cloak closer, shivering as the night air made its way through her skirts and made her hair cling to her neck. Something in the air was unfriendly: even the laughter that came from taverns and boats made her uneasy. Tomas hardly seemed mindful of it. He strode through the streets like a king at home in his own country and stopped at the base of the clock tower.

The door to the tower was tall, wide, and locked with some twenty locks, bolts, and chains. Celine stared at it in dismay.

Tomas looked back at her and smiled. "My home welcomes you," he said. "Hospitable as ever, as you can see."

Without a word of warning he threw Grandfather Monk over his shoulder, grabbed one of the chains with one hand, and started to climb the door. Celine watched as he nimbly made his way up the door, onto a ledge, around a corner, and up still more. He disappeared from sight.

She was alone in the street. The clammy air seemed somehow more threatening; the city noises closer at hand. She swallowed and tried to pretend she wasn't afraid. The moon had been dreadful and lonely, but dreadful because it was lonely. Nothing there had actually threatened her. This was different.

There was a swoop in the darkness, and something plummeted down before her. She nearly screamed. She put her hand over her heart, willing it to stop pounding as though it would break right through her ribcage. It was only Tomas. He had jumped down from some unseen height.

"Your turn," he said.

Before she knew to protest, he had thrown her over his shoulder as easily as he had Grandfather Monk. She opened her mouth to complain, but he was halfway up the door before she could, and she was looking down on the streets from a dizzying height. He moved fast, practically jumping higher and higher, and the street below rocked and spun and threatened to pull her back.

She closed her eyes tightly and willed the climb to be over. In another moment, it was. She felt herself being lowered onto dry, slightly dusty boards, and she opened her eyes to a strange little world that could only belong to someone like Tomas.

They were in a large room behind the clock face. The faint lights of the city and the celestial lights above the sea glowed through it, casting a warm sheen on everything. Candles of various heights, widths, and colours stood in stands scattered throughout the room, and Tomas was even now lighting them. More were balanced on a chandelier that hung from a rafter overhead. The massive iron clockworks rose from the center of the floor, gears and wires moving slowly with faint groans.

All around them an odd collection of artifacts lay, sat, and stood, forming an oddly welcoming architecture in the glowing lights. Globes and telescopes, maps and musty old books in stacks. Small clocks that kept time with the clock tower—all but one, Celine noted, which had stopped working. A model ship the size of a small dog hung from another rafter, seeming to sail through the dusty air. On one wall, a huge painting hung. It showed a castle on a ridge in craggy green mountains, the sun setting behind it. As Celine looked closer she realized that the painting had once been in thousands of tiny pieces: it was a puzzle, pieced together carefully over a span of time.

The pryoline mewed and stretched itself out on the floorboards. A sigh escaped Celine. There was something so old and eccentric and welcoming about this place that she couldn't help herself. In the next moment she remembered how she'd reached the top of the tower, and she whirled around and glared at Tomas.

"Don't you ever do that again," she said.

"It's a long climb," he answered. He was arranging Grandfather Monk on a long red couch.

"One I'm perfectly capable of making on my own," she said.

Tomas said nothing. She had the distinct feeling that he was smiling—smiling to himself in amusement at her. Celine was accustomed to being a nuisance, an interruption, and a thorn in her uncle's side. She was not accustomed to being an amusement, and the feeling rankled her.

Vexed, she opened her mouth to level a few choice words at Tomas, but he had stood and appeared startlingly by her side. His face was placid and pleasant. "Listen," he said.

She shut her mouth and did as he said. Beneath the groan of the clockworks and the gentle snores of Grandfather Monk, through the glass face of the clock and its light layer of dust, she heard a gentle pulse: a heartbeat, a distant song.

"What is it?" she asked.

"The sea," he said.

She closed her eyes for a moment. There in the clock tower of Meru, overlooking the harbours of the bay, she heard what a thousand sailors had heard before her. The call of the sea. The allure of wave and deep, of endlessly moving stillness, of a world that reflected back the sky. Something deep inside her answered it back.

She opened her eyes again. Tomas had moved: he'd climbed halfway up the gears and was sitting on a slowly rotating wooden platform, staring out through the glass of the clock face. It was opaque, barely see-through-able, but his eyes imagined the sea and drew it for her. She felt as though she could look out over the reaches of water and of ages.

All the way home.

"How long," she said, her voice sounding strangely in the tower, "does it take to cross the sea?"

He looked down at her with mild surprise. "Where do you want to go?" he asked.

"Home." Impatience rose in her slightly. "I told you I wanted to go."

He shook his head. "I wish you wouldn't."

"Should that matter to me?" she asked.

He looked down at her and tilted his golden head, half-orange in the candlelight. "Does it?" he asked.

The question caught her off guard. It did matter—for some reason. She formed her words carefully, almost stumbling over them. "Look—Tomas—you've been good and kind to me. You rescued me from the moon, and I won't forget it. And I'm thankful you brought me here. Truly."

She looked around her as she spoke. Something about the strange surroundings would be with her forever. This was a world of its own—a small world hinting at all the discoveries and longings and excitement of a greater world, with its maps and telescopes and forever-setting suns in oil paint.

She continued. "But I have to go home."

He said nothing. Only looked down at her from his perch on the wooden platform, one knee drawn up near his chin. She looked up at him and sighed.

"My home is mine," she said. "It needs me. And I wasn't alone there—I had a friend. She needs me. Even my uncle needs me. I have to go back."

Tomas kept looking down at her. His eyes were strangely conflicted.

"How long?" she asked, gesturing toward the glass clock face and the sea beyond it.

"Years," he said. "The sea is wide. No ship will take you directly to your old home. It would take years to get back."

Dismay struck her. "I can't wait years!" she said.

"Of course you can't," he said. He looked down at his feet. "I know that."

He jumped down suddenly, landing on the plank floor more lightly than any man should be able to. The pyroline got up and twisted itself around his legs.

"If you go back," he said, "we'll need to use the rings again."

The word "we" was just registering in her head when he looked at her, catching her off guard with the strength in his eyes, and said, "We'll talk about it in the morning."

And without another word, he gestured to a feather mattress tucked between stacks of old books, turned on his heel, clambered back up the clockworks, and disappeared in the highest reaches of the tower. Celine looked down at the feather mattress. It was surprisingly clean, and a fantastically woven blanket of blue and white and bright pink lay at the foot of it. Suddenly all the candles and the air with its smells of wood and oil and iron seemed to be urging her to sleep. She lay down, pulled the blanket over her, and succumbed to her surroundings.

Late that night, Celine awoke. The light of the moon had grown stronger. It streamed through the glass of the clock face and glinted off a sword blade.

Tomas held the sword. It was slender, slim, deadly. Fire seemed to dance in its length. Celine found herself growing slowly terrified as she looked at it. All the worse was that it was in Tomas's hands. It ought not to be—nothing so full of death ought to be.

He was looking at it pensively, moving it up and down so the moonlight played off the blade. He looked up suddenly and saw her watching him. She tried to decipher the words in his eyes, but she couldn't. They were sad, strangely knowing.

Without a word, he sheathed the sword. The room grew darker. He turned and disappeared in the shadows, taking the terror of the blade with him.

Celine woke up, as she often did, with a question on her tongue.

"Were you really on the moon for ninety-three years?" she asked the soaring shadows above her, barely touched by the sun's rays through the clock face.

After a moment, there was movement in the heights. With a rattle, Tomas dropped downward, holding lightly to a chain. He stopped himself ten feet above her.

"I told you I was," he said.

"Yes, I know," Celine said. "But I didn't believe you. You don't look a day over twenty."

Tomas looked amused. "Why do you believe me now?" he asked.

Celine nodded at the scarlet couch. "Because Grandfather Monk wouldn't lie, and his wrinkles can't. It was really you he saw disappear ninety-three years ago?"

"I'm afraid I went without much warning," Tomas said. "I didn't expect the rings to act quite so . . . suddenly. Not that I wanted to stay. The people in that village kept trying to make me into something I'm not."

"God," Celine said.

He nodded, swinging thoughtfully from the chain. "Yes."

Celine sat up, running her fingers through her long hair

to comb out a few snarls. "What exactly are you?"

He smiled down at her. "I'm an Immortal."

She paused. The words in her mouth tasted strange, even though she'd thought them more than once since meeting Tomas—not in the beginning, of course, because she really hadn't believed him about the ninety-three years. But the more she watched him, the more obvious it was. He formed shapes out of rain and memories and lifted strong men without effort. Not to mention, she thought as the fire-cat shook off the edge of her blanket and emerged blinking into the early morning sunlight, he kept company with pyrolines.

"You're just like my uncle," she said.

Tomas grimaced. "He's an Immortal too," he said. "Yes."

"But," Celine pressed on, "aren't Immortals usually consumed with some purpose? My uncle has never sat still a day in his life—at least, not in all the life I've ever seen, or heard of. He's always building his collection and becoming better at . . . at all the things he does. You seem to be determined to do nothing but waste time."

Tomas slid down the rest of the chain and dropped himself onto the floorboards. "That's not quite fair," he said. "I'm not trying to waste my time so much as I'm trying to avoid using it."

"That," Celine informed him, "doesn't make any sense."

"Oh, it does," he told her. His expression was graver than she'd seen yet. "Much more than you know."

With a grunt and a groan, Grandfather Monk woke himself. The sun, gorgeous yellow through the clock face, was shining in his eyes. He tried to say something, but it came out as an incoherent garble. His waking galvanized both Tomas and Celine to action. Celine was at his feet in a moment, rubbing them. Tomas jumped like one with a fire beneath him to a small cookstove in the midst of his paraphernalia, where he was soon cooking up a pot of porridge. Where he'd acquired oats that weren't rotted and dissolved with age Celine didn't know. Perhaps he'd shaped them out of memory; perhaps he'd collected them unobserved in the Fallow Fields.

When they were finished, Tomas invited Grandfather Monk to sit up and partake.

The old man sighed wheezily. His watery eyes were droopier than usual. "I fear not," he said. "Can't sit up . . . can't quite seem to move."

Celine frowned. "Are you all right?" she asked.

"No, no," Monk answered. "No and yes."

"You're not dying?" Tomas asked.

Monk didn't seem to think the question strange. "I'm afraid so," he said. "About time, after all. I'm nearing one hundred."

"But you can't die!" Celine burst out. "It's not fair. We only just met you. We only just got here!"

Tomas pulled a stool up by the old man's head and leaned forward intently. "Couldn't you take a few more years?" he asked. "You've beaten all the odds so far. Keep it up a little while longer." The light in his face seemed to grow as he spoke. "I'll stay and tend you . . . the whole time. I promise I will."

Celine stood. She was upset and couldn't hide it, so she turned away from the men and tried to calm herself down. She wasn't sure what upset her most: the calm way both men seemed to accept death, the loss of a man she'd decided to love, or Tomas's selfishness. "A little while longer," he'd said. He only wanted Monk to live so he could keep avoiding whatever he was avoiding.

But, after all, Monk *did* seem determined to die. And, after all, he was a very old man.

When she turned back, Tomas was feeding Monk with a long-handled spoon. There was something beautiful about them: the shining young man and the old one who looked back at his benefactor with something close to worship. Celine wanted suddenly to cry.

"It's not fair," she repeated.

"It's all right," Tomas said. He sounded very sure of himself, and really very pleased. His tone of voice made him impossible not to believe. "It will be years yet. You don't mind, do you?" he asked Monk. "Living years more?"

"Well," Monk said, "not if you're in them."

"Oh, I'll be here," Tomas said. "We'll take care of you."

There was that "we" again. Celine bristled at it. It wasn't fair of him—not at all. "Not me," she said.

Tomas looked up at her with a stricken face. He evidently hadn't expected her to object.

"I have to go home," she said. "I told you that. Grandfather—I'm sorry."

He tried to smile. "Quite all right," he said. "Quite all right."

"It's not all right," Tomas said. He was almost frowning now. "You can't go back."

Celine found herself wishing—again—for something to throw at him. "I told you last night I can't stay here. I'm needed. I—I'd like to stay. You know it, and you're trying to use that against me. But I can't. There are prior claims."

"Your prior claims banished you!" Tomas said. He still looked stricken.

Celine looked at him for a long moment. "That doesn't change anything," she said.

She turned away again. She reached in her pocket and pulled out her ring. The sun danced on it. As she looked, the inside of it started to glimmer as it had done on the moon. Rainbow colours, fairy glimmer. Soap-bubble beauty, in something that was at once simple and dangerous.

What would happen, she wondered, if she used the ring wrongly? If she didn't wait for Tomas. If she tried to go on her own.

Celine was nothing if not strong-willed. She had forced her will through by temper, bravado, and scrub brush more times than she could count. And will, she knew, always had some power with magic. That was why willful people couldn't really be trusted with it.

She slipped her finger in the ring.

And disappeared.

Strange as it is to watch someone disappear, it is even stranger to disappear to yourself. For a few moments Celine could not find herself. Her body was gone, and her spirit felt a little unsteady itself. She wasn't in darkness or enveloped in a flash of light. She just—wasn't.

A moment later she was standing in a garden she recognized. It was an old, overgrown garden, in a part of her uncle's palace that no one tended anymore. It was the part of the palace where her mother had died.

The pyrolines, huge, lionlike, and breathing smoke, were stalking around her.

Chapter 5

TOMAS JUMPED TO HIS FEET at Celine's disappearance. He knew what had happened at once. "Blast those rings!" he said.

Grandfather Monk tugged at his sleeve. He looked down. He'd nearly upset the bowl of porridge in his surprise.

"She's gone?" Monk asked.

"Blast her," Tomas answered.

"In trouble?" Monk asked. "She is, isn't she? Girls as beautiful as that are always in trouble."

Tomas looked miserable. The expression wasn't at all suited to his features; it made him look like a grubby boy. "I'm afraid so."

"Well," Monk said. "Go after her."

Tomas sat down and put his head in his hands. "I can't," he said.

"I'll wait," Monk said. Tomas felt movement beside him. He opened his eyes and lifted his head. Monk was slowly pushing himself off the couch. He took a few shuffling steps toward the cookstove. "Food and fuel all there?" he asked. "Enough to keep me a while?"

Tomas nodded. "A good while."

"I'll wait for you," Monk said. "Won't die till you get back. I promise."

"But—" Tomas began.

The old man looked at him with surprising force, then laid himself back on the couch and folded his hands in his middle. "I've been waiting for you all my life," he said. "I can hold on a bit longer. Go save the girl."

Celine was so tense she felt as though anything could snap her. The pyrolines stared at her with evil glowing eyes as they circled around. Fear pounded in her throat. They were creatures of prey—cruel things trained up by her uncle. She had never, ever wanted to be the prey.

Through her fear, tears of frustration stung her eyes. She was so close to coming home safely. It was so bad that they should stop her here. Stop her like this.

A voice cut through her fear, one that roused several emotions in her at once. Relief, of course, for it meant she was rescued. But where her heart rose with relief, her stomach sank with dread—and then steeled itself. The voice belonged to Ignus Umbria.

"Off with you," the voice said. The pyrolines hissed their displeasure, but they moved aside. Their long, golden fur, tipped with black, bristled. They kept their eyes on Celine, but the tension in her muscles slowly relaxed. They might have eaten her without a moment's regret, but the creatures dared not cross her uncle.

She lifted her eyes to her uncle's face, straightening her back and holding her head high as she did so, positioning every inch of herself in dignity and composure.

Ignus Umbria was not a large man. He was in fact just shorter than Celine, with a curving spine and slightly bowed legs. His face was dark, long, and pinched, with jowls that managed to hang despite the fact that he hadn't a bit of extra fat on him. His eyes were black and intense, always piercing, searching, and lighting up with excitement over new discoveries. His hands, which he held one in the other before him as though he were regarding a feast, were those of an artist, with long, fine, sensitive fingers. They were nearly as beautiful as Celine's own hands, a fact which had made her realize in the past that beauty can be especially hideous when it's used wrongly.

"So you're back," he said. "Is that fool following you?"

The question caught her off guard. She had expected

him to rant and rave over her return if he was in a bad mood, to treat it as no great event if he was in a good one. In any case she had expected to be back scrubbing floors by the afternoon. His piercing glare on her now was not what she had expected, and it made her uncomfortable.

"Who are you talking about?" she asked.

Her uncle cackled. "That fool on the moon. The one whose house I burned down."

Too late Celine remembered the Ravening Fire, and how she had wondered why her uncle would target the hut of a man like Tomas. It struck her very suddenly and very hard that she'd gotten herself into the middle of something.

"He's not coming here," she said. She held her voice remarkably steady.

"He will," Umbria answered. He looked past her and crooked a finger.

The guards materialized out of the shrubbery. They were Umbria's own particular sort of guards: plant-men with fingers that left spots like poison ivy wherever they touched. They seized Celine's arm with the strength of old and deeply rooted trees. She tried to pull herself away, but to no avail.

"What is the meaning of this?" she demanded. "What do you think you're doing?"

"Making good use of you," Umbria answered. "You're not a bad floor-scrubber, but you'll do me a better service cooling that lovely head in the dungeon a while."

Celine turned pale despite her anger. "I don't under-stand," she said. "What possible reason—"

"Don't be stupid, my dear," Umbria interrupted. "You make very pretty bait. I give him three days. If he's not storm-ing my castle by then, he's no true Immortal."

He cackled to himself, wringing his beautiful hands in self-congratulation. He nodded curtly to the plant-men.

"Take her away," he said.

Tomas disliked losing himself to the rings. For him the journey seemed to take much longer than it had for Celine. He was, in fact, far more sensitive to the passage of time. He had spent much of his immortality trying to drag out his days, and he had become very adept at it. To him the loss of body and presence was disturbing in many ways.

When he came back together all in one piece, he found himself inside a cave. For a bare instant he thought he was back on the moon, but then he realized he couldn't be: there was water dripping from the rock ceiling. The moon had been a very dry place, dry and dusty and cold. This place was wet and strangely warm. Moss was growing up the sides of it.

Fresh air was flowing to him from the west, and he thought he saw a glimmer of sunlight. He followed it un-til he found a small hole just wide enough for his head and shoulders to pass through. The rest of him being long and lanky as it was, he emerged blinking into the sun without any trouble.

He was on a hillside. Most of the hill stretched out below him, yards upon yards of it. It was green and dotted with white rocks. The hill climbed up another twenty feet or so and then ended in a meeting with the blue sky. There were no paths or roads in any direction that he could see, nor did the countryside seem at all inhabited. For a moment he entertained the wild fear that the ring had sent him somewhere as desolate as the Fallow Fields—and as far away from helping Celine.

That moment quickly ended. From somewhere over the top of the hill the sound of a sheep loudly baaing interrupted his fears. He scrambled up the hill toward the sound.

The hill ended in a flat, grassy ridge that almost immediately sloped down again on the other side. And the other side, to his great delight, was covered with sheep. In the middle of them, laying in the grass with his bare toes in the air, was a shepherd. His age or size Tomas could only guess. Little was visible of him beneath the grass and the pressing, wooly crowd but bare toes and a straw hat.

Farther away, up and over another ridge, were the spires of a palace—the palace, Tomas was nearly certain, of Ignus Umbria. The ring had done its job after all.

A fat sheep with wool that sprung out thickly from every inch of its body, allowing only its nose to poke out, looked up at Tomas and baaed in protest of his presence. Tomas looked down at his feet and discovered that he was standing in a particularly succulent patch of grass. He jumped aside with a quick apology.

In response, the shepherd's bare toes disappeared, and a head poked up from the grass. The face was shaded by the oversized hat, but it was a youthful face, not handsome but full of character. The eyes that looked out beneath the brim were the colour of wheat.

"Heigh," the shepherd called. "Where did ye come from?"

He didn't wait for an answer, scrambling to his feet and snatching up his shepherd's crook. He wielded it like a spear, poking one end in Tomas's direction. "Keep your distance!"

Tomas held up both his hands. "I'm no threat to you," he said.

"It's not t'me I'm worried about," the shepherd boy answered. "It's them sheep. Keep off!"

Tomas raised his hands a little higher. The boy had come up the hill and was now moving back and forth like a guard before a gate. He was small and compact, probably fifteen or so years old. His shoulders and arms looked strong through his dirty white shirt. His feet were wide and calloused. He whistled without taking his eyes off Tomas. A bark answered him, and a black-and-white head popped up from the grass. A moment later the sheepdog stood. It was a fine animal with long, feathery fur and intelligent green eyes.

"Ye're a worthless animal!" the shepherd boy called as the dog joined him, still not taking his eyes from Tomas. "What d'ye mean lazing in the grass all the while? Ye see yon fellow? That's a thief! Get the thief!"

The dog smiled up at his master, wagged his tail, and didn't move. The boy cursed. "Stupid creeture!"

Tomas couldn't help smiling. The dog had sized him up far more accurately than the boy. Immortals and animals always did read each other well.

"He's not afraid of me," Tomas said. "He knows I mean no harm. I'll just be on my way, if you'll allow me."

The boy looked suspiciously at Tomas. "Where are ye going?" he asked. "Ye look a thief to me. Dressed like a scarecrow and coming up over a hill where never man comes over."

Tomas pointed at the ridge beyond and the palace spires rising behind it. "To the palace," he said.

The boy nearly dropped his crook with surprise. "Umbria's palace? I wouldn't go there. Na, I wouldn't go there a'tall. Bad business happening there and no mistake."

"What kind of bad business?" Tomas asked.

The boy shook his head. "Smokings and groanings. Weird lights and somethin' in the sky at night that's bigger than any bird ever was. Big as a ship, it is. The villagers won't look at it. They're all afrighted."

"Are you afraid?" Tomas asked. It occurred to him suddenly that this lad might be just the sort of person he needed.

The boy held his crook a little defensively again. "Not me," he said. "Brig and I, we're afraid of nothing." He waved to the sheep on the hillside. "Ye see these fool creetures? They're Umbria's sheep. I keeps them for him. Won't no one else touch his flocks, but I've no fear."

"I'm glad to hear it," Tomas said. "I want you to take me to the palace and help me find a way in."

The boy turned a funny shade. Not white, but something close to it. "Not on your life," he said. "I'm no coward, but I'm no fool neither."

Tomas sighed. He had hoped. He started forward, but the boy stopped him by poking him in the stomach with the end of his shepherd's crook.

"Ye're not going in there," he said. "Not yet."

Tomas straightened himself, rubbing the spot the crook had hit. "I have to get in there."

"Wait," the boy answered. "Ye can wait, can't ye? Nothing needs doing that won't wait a few more hours. When was the last time you were in those walls?"

"Never," Tomas confessed. His conscience pricked slightly. It was the truth, but hardly the answer he should be giving.

"Well then," the boy said, rolling the crook in his palm, "ye don't know what ye're facing. I tell you something's going on in there. Whatever it 'tis sails through the sky at night; ye'll face it. Don't ye want to know your enemy?"

There was wisdom in the boy's words, that much Tomas had to concede. It occurred to him suddenly that his determined dallying might have given Umbria a great deal of time to grow strong. An image of Celine within the castle walls flickered into his mind, and his conscience ceased pricking and started to prod in earnest. He wondered what she was doing. Had Umbria put her back to floor-scrubbing, or had he—as Tomas suspected—greeted her even less cordially than that?

A knowing look had come into the boy's eyes. "Well then," he said. "Lay out on this hillside tonight. Don't sleep. Watch, and see what ye can see."

"I'll do it," Tomas said. The necessary delay galled him, but the boy was right. Only a fool would walk into Umbria's palace without a clue of what he was up against. "Tell me," he said, "is there a way I can look into the palace without Umbria seeing me?"

The boy looked from side to side as though he feared someone would overhear him. He lowered his voice. "There's a way," he said. "But it's not everyone can be using it."

Tomas lowered his own voice to match. "Can I be using it?" he asked.

The boy leaned forward and stared at Tomas for a long, unnerving minute. The wheat-coloured eyes were unusually probing. Tomas wondered what he had gotten himself into. Finally, the boy nodded.

"Ye can," he said. He thrust his crook forward and prodded Tomas in the ribs, hard. As a protest escaped Tomas's lips, the boy said, "But if ye betray us, ye'll regret it as long as ye live."

Chapter 6

HE SHEPHERD BOY, WHOSE NAME WAS ALDON, left his sheep in the care of the dog Brig and led Tomas away. He walked with a sturdy pace, thudding his shepherd's crook on the ground with every step. They descended the ridge, skirted a small forest, and entered the dusty streets of a village full of chickens, old women, and shops that seemed designed to be boarded tightly at a moment's notice. No one paid them much mind, including the chickens, who squawked, flapped, and got underfoot. Aldon broke up a gang of them with the end of his crook and a solid bare heel.

It was not a small village. Toward the center of it, old buildings rose up in strange spires, looking as though they stood sentry from a distant age. Streets wound off in many directions, most dirt, some haphazardly cobbled. Aldon took one of the latter. Buildings packed closely together leaned over the street, casting it into shadow and coming closer until they seemed bent on choking it out altogether.

At the very end of it, three steps led down to a cracked oak door.

Aldon knocked on the door with the end of his crook and bent low with his ear almost against the wood, waiting. Tomas stood at the top of the stairs, wishing the sun would shine a little more freely into the street. There was a spirit about the shadows that he didn't like.

A muffled voice from the other side of the door called, "Who's there?"

"Aldon," the shepherd boy answered. "Let us in."

For a moment nothing happened. Then the door opened just wide enough for a blue eye to peer out over a series of chain links. The eye fixed itself on Tomas.

"Who's he?"

"A friend," Aldon said. "Ye can trust him. Let us come in, woman; 'tis cold out here."

The day was a warm one, and the sun was still high in the sky. Yet Tomas agreed wholeheartedly with Aldon's words. In a way that went deeper than skin and sunshine, it was cold in the street.

The door slammed shut. There was a sound of chains and bolts being drawn, and in the next moment the door flung open. A woman with flaming red hair stood with her back against it, motioning for them to come in. She swept the street with her sharp blue eyes, daring something to jump out of the shadows. Nothing did. As soon as Tomas and Aldon were through the door, she slammed it behind them and commenced rebolting and chaining it against the world outside. From the back, as she bent down to draw the lowermost chains, she looked less like a woman than like a bundle of rags wrapped around a few thin branches.

She stood and turned faster than Tomas would have thought possible, impaling him with her eyes.

She was not at all pretty. Her face was sharp and striking. She was the skinniest woman he had ever seen: somewhere between the ages of twenty and thirty but built like sticks tied together at the joints. She wore many layers of clothing, cinched up tightly at the waist and shoulders and several times down her arms. Her boots were black and several sizes too big.

Her eyes were remarkable, like Aldon's, but different. They flickered away from Tomas and lighted on the shepherd.

"Well," she said. "There's bread in the pantry."

He didn't bother thanking her, but opened a bin in one corner of the little apartment and came out holding a loaf of sourdough. He ripped off a piece and started to work on it.

"Hungry?" the woman asked Tomas.

He shook his head. Aldon drew alongside him, talking with his mouth full. "He wants in to Umbria's house," he said. "Got business there."

Her eyes flashed. "Ever been?" she asked.

He shook his head again.

"Watch yourself, then," she said. "Dark things in that house. Always have been, but now especially."

Tomas waited for Aldon to tell her that they planned to lay out on the hillside and watch for at least one of those dark things. He knew without being told that this woman and the shepherd boy had a deep bond of trust. But Aldon said nothing.

"I have to go in," Tomas said. "I don't expect it to be easy. Aldon told me that if we came here, I could see into the palace."

Her eyes glittered. "Have to use magic," she said. "Does that scare you?"

He smiled. It was the first time he'd done so since entering the apartment. "I didn't expect to look out the window and see it."

She almost cackled. "Close, though," she said. "Very close."

She turned and began to take down a blanket that was draped over the wall, tacked up in the corners with half-driven nails. It was so dark in the apartment that Tomas hadn't noticed it at first. As one corner fell, a head appeared behind it. He started before he realized that it was his own. He was looking into a mirror.

"There," the woman said, putting her hands on her bony hips in satisfaction. "Umbria's own looking glass. Enchanted it himself."

Tomas smiled again as he stepped closer to the huge

glass pane. "And how did you come to have it?" he asked.

"How do you think?" the woman answered. "I stole it with my own two hands."

For some reason, he hadn't expected that. "Then you've been in the palace?"

"Many's a time," she answered. "I scrubbed floors there when I was a girl."

"Are there many floors to scrub?" Tomas asked. His eyes were still on the looking glass. His reflection was beginning to blur.

She snorted. "Acres of them."

Tomas took his eyes away from the strangely altering reflection. "What is your name?" he asked.

"Tereska," she answered. Somewhere in the back of the room, a bird squawked.

He turned back to the looking glass. The scene reflected in it began to blur: first the dark apartment, with Tereska and Aldon standing at the edges so that his own face stood out sharply in contrast. Then the lines of his head started to blur: his golden shock of hair, his eyebrows, his ears and chin. Nose and mouth faded, and he stared into his own eyes, more brilliant than they had ever been.

Then they blinked out. The mirror was dark.

In the next instant it flared to life again. Tomas saw the tall spires of the palace glimmering in the sun. The view swept dizzily down, as though it was seen through the eyes of a bird in a tailspin. It fixed on a large rectangular courtyard, with gardens spotting it and a huge fountain in the center that cast up water in high, foamy spurts. The view came down all the way to the flagstones of the courtyard and stopped there, as though the bird had cast itself to its death on the the ground. Then the view righted itself, taking in the sweep of the walls and the many doors, tall and rounded at the tops, painted red and green and gold. A cricket hopped across the stones. The view focused on it. Then the view hopped forward twice, pounced on the cricket, and ate it.

"It is a bird!" Tomas exclaimed.

"The looking glass needs eyes," Tereska said, as though she was explaining something extremely obvious to someone extremely stupid.

Tomas almost protested. A bird wasn't good enough. He needed to see inside the palace, beyond the courtyard— to Umbria's chambers, or the place where the dark danger lurked, or some other place he could use. Or Celine. If he could just see Celine, he would be happy.

The view hopped forward again, looking up and around jerkily. "Fly," Tomas muttered. At least if the bird flew, he could get a better overview of the place—and the vision wouldn't jerk around so much.

To his surprise, the bird obeyed. He smiled. Of course. Strong will always influenced magic—the looking glass was no different, even if it was using a bird. The view flapped up and landed on top of the fountain.

"Not there!" Tomas exclaimed. In the next instant a geyser of water shot up, covering the looking glass in water.

The bird tried to fly away, but its movements were obviously weighed down. The view was soggy, sporadic, blinking out.

The vision came back in again, still wet, but drying. The bird had flown up to light on the rounded archway over one of the doors. The courtyard lay before it. It had a wide view, for which Tomas was grateful. He had the distinct feeling that the creature was shaking out its feathers.

A moment later, a door across the courtyard burst open, and four tall, leafy guards came through. They had a struggling, clearly unhappy Celine between them. She pulled one arm free and landed a blow on a guard's shoulder, but he grabbed her again and marched on, impervious. Tomas strained to see more clearly. At least she didn't appear harmed. The guards marched her across the courtyard, opened a door of deep purple, and dragged her through.

Two seconds later the view dove back to the flagstones and gobbled up another cricket.

Tomas turned away from the looking glass. "Where does that door lead?" he asked Tereska.

"Dungeon," she said.

He turned back to the looking glass, but his own face was all that looked back. He'd broken the magic by turning away.

"Is it . . . what sort of dungeon?" Tomas asked.

"The usual sort," she answered. Once again her tone was scornful. "Wet, stinking, not much light. A few rats. Lots of crickets."

"What are those guards?" he asked.

"Rosebushes, I think," Tereska answered. "Or they were. I got out before Umbria finished that experiment."

It suddenly occurred to Tomas that Tereska could be of far more use than any bird's-eye view, given by a magic mirror or not.

"Would you . . ." he began.

She shook her head. "No. You want to go in there, you go in there alone. I'm not risking it." His face must have expressed more misery than he thought, because her sharp expression softened a little. "I'm not much of a hand for drawing," she said. "But I'll draw you a map."

He smiled. "Thank you."

Aldon looked up from his loaf of sourdough. "Tereska, have ye a few dark cloaks left?"

"Two," she answered. She frowned at Aldon. "What d'you want with them?"

Aldon shrugged. "Could be useful." He didn't look her in the face. She squinted at him a moment longer, and then understanding dawned.

"No," she said. "No. You're not going out there tonight."

Aldon looked up with his eyes suddenly fierce. "Are ye afraid?" he asked.

"Yes," Tereska said. She marched across the room and started to tack the blanket back up over the looking glass. "You've no business risking yourself now, Aldon. We're not ready."

"All the planning in the world won't help us if we don't learn what the shadow is," Aldon argued. "The dark cloaks will hide us."

She glared at him. "You hope. And if they don't? If they don't I'm left alone."

"If we go in there and face it together without knowing what it is, 'twill eat us both alive. Much good your planning will do ye."

Tomas interrupted. "Let me see the dark cloaks."

Tereska shot him a look, but she obeyed. She opened a trunk and pulled out a black length of material, spotted with bits of green. As her hands touched it, it seemed to lose substance, melting into the shadows of the room. She passed it over. It was silky and heavy in his hands. He turned it, watching with pleasure as it changed colour to blend with its surroundings.

"Stole this too, did you?" Tomas asked.

"Yes," Tereska said.

"I've never seen finer," he said. "Whatever you need to hide from, these will do the trick or nothing will."

Aldon gave Tereska a triumphant nod. "That's settled, then."

She took the cloak back, looking dubiously at both of them. "All right," she said. Then she drew herself up and glared at Tomas. "I'll not have you thinking me a common thief," she said. "You might say these things were stolen first from me."

Tomas cocked his head. "What do you mean?"

"My father was a gifted man," she said. "A weaver, a carpenter, a glassmaker, and a blacksmith. Umbria hired him to come and furnish his house, but he never paid for any of it. Not for these cloaks, not for that mirror. My father grew ill and died in Umbria's house, and I went to work scrubbing floors while the lord of the house played with magic."

"And now?" Tomas asked. "Why are you still here? Hiding in the darkness . . . why don't you go away, somewhere Umbria can't find you?"

Her blue eyes flashed. "Half the finery in his house belongs to me," she said. "I want it back."

"And you?" Tomas asked Aldon. "What are you planning, you who aren't afraid to shepherd for the man? What conspiracy is this that binds you two together?"

Aldon glared at him. "Never a word," he said. "Never a word to any man."

"I'm no friend of Ignus Umbria's," Tomas said. "I won't cross you."

Aldon sniffed. "My great-great-great-grandfather was lord of these parts once. He made all the people free and gave up his lordship. 'Twas his dream to see all men equal, but Umbria came and made everyone slaves to fear."

"You want to carry out his dream?" Tomas asked.

"Yes," Aldon said. "And my father's, and his father's."

Tomas looked between the two: the stocky teenage shepherd and the rail-thin, fiery-haired washerwoman. "And you two are it?" he said. "The whole rebellion unto yourselves? There's no one else to help you?"

Tereska raised her chin. "We'll manage," she said.

Tomas smiled. "I believe you will," he said. "But you'll never defeat Umbria. Not alone."

Aldon's eyes flashed. "And who else do we need, I ask ye?" he said.

Tomas met his gaze. "Me," he said.

Chapter 7

CELINE SAT WITH HER KNEES DRAWN UP to her chest and her back inches from the cold stone wall. Water dripped down the wall in small, evenly spaced rivulets, making it impossible to lean against without growing progressively soaked. The water did not pool on the floor, which gave Celine to know that it was one of her uncle's experiments—dampness, after all, being essential to a proper dungeon.

The floor was a little slimy anyhow, as green algae was growing on it. It glowed slightly. A window high in the wall let a tiny bit of light in, but the light was growing dimmer as evening approached. Celine alternated between quiet raging and creeping despair. Her uncle couldn't do this to her, of course. It wasn't right. It wasn't decent. It wasn't fair! But, then again, he was doing it.

And somehow she'd gotten herself in between her uncle and Tomas. And Tomas would come here. She tried to deny it, but he would. Tomas was the sort of man who came after you when you did stupid, headstrong things. He was the sort of man who got friends out of trouble when they got themselves into it. And he was Immortal, which meant that everything he was, he was more than other people.

She rested her head on her arms, burying her face slightly. She kept remembering the first question he'd asked her. Marry him. She'd wondered why he'd asked it, because she didn't really believe he was in love. She hadn't believed he'd spent ninety-three years on the moon, either, but she'd been wrong. Now she really, really hoped that whatever he felt for her, it wasn't love.

Love made people do stupid things. Tomas was Immortal, so if he was in love, his stupidity was probably immense enough to tear the world down around their ears.

Celine picked up a piece of rock and hurled it across the cell with all her might. It bounced off the wall and skittered across the floor within her reach. Again.

Celine looked up to the window. The fading light brought her some hope, at least. With her eyes trained on the opening, she whistled the first three bars of a tune.

It was a moderately fast song, a little sad but not too much. She'd loved the song for years before it became a signal.

Nothing happened. She waited a few minutes and whistled it again.

A slight sound from above encouraged her. She whistled louder.

Something green and leafy passed by the window. She cut her song off. The guard made no sign that it had heard her.

She waited. Ten minutes. Fifteen. The cell was almost completely dark; the world above hushed in twilight. The guards made no more sounds in the courtyard.

Slowly, she started to whistle the tune one more time. Unreasonable fear struck her. What if something had happened?

What if no one was there to hear her signal?

The idea wasn't to be born. She forced it down and finished the tune, only wavering slightly in the middle.

And then something dark stuck its head through the middle bar and blinked down at her out of a grey, furry face. She almost cheered.

"Get down here!" she stage-whispered.

The head disappeared. A few pebbles fell through the window, and a moment later the back legs appeared, showing off sharp claws, a round grey rump, and a barely-there stub of a tail. The back legs scrabbled for a hold on the stone wall as the creature started to lower itself in—more like a human than like an animal. The claws scratched against the stones and failed to find anything. A moment later the front claws lost their grip and the creature plummeted. Celine jumped out and grabbed it.

The little creature, about the size of a kitten but much more bearlike, turned itself around and cuddled down against her, quivering both with delight and fear. Celine rubbed her fingers between its miniature rabbit-like ears and held it up so she could kiss the flat nose.

"Be more careful next time, Winnie," she said.

The creature blinked at her and said, "What are you doing here? I thought you were on the moon!"

"I was," Celine said. "I came back."

"Back to the dungeon," Winnie said, wiggling herself loose and dropping into Celine's lap. She curled up in Celine's skirt and scratched her snout with her long claws. "Iggy must be mad. You should have seen him hooting and dancing when he sent you off. I thought he was going to slip and break something."

"But he didn't?" Celine asked.

"No, sadly."

Celine stroked the little creature's back. "How is life?"

Winnie wrinkled her nose. "There've been some nice chestnuts lately . . . better than all those roots all summer. Still trying to keep out of notice. I'm glad to be a twilight animal. The pyrolines don't see well in the twilight, and those leafy things don't hear me because the wind rustles through them so loudly. Do you know, Celine? They look tasty."

Celine laughed. "I hope you haven't tried eating them."

"I've been tempted. Life is all eating, for a wombat. Even

a miniature one like me. But I didn't want to get caught . . . not when I didn't know if you'd be back."

"You're a faithful friend," Celine said.

"But Celine," Winnie said, her tone growing suddenly serious, "something's going on around here. Iggy's got something up his sleeve and I . . . I don't come out at night anymore."

"Why?" Celine asked, frowning. "What do you do, stay in your burrow all the time?"

Winnie nodded, the action strange for a marsupial. "Something comes out at night that makes all my instincts tingle. I'm scared of it. I don't dare come out."

"Well," Celine said, "you can stay with me now. No one's likely to see you down here."

"Good," Winnie said. She looked up, black beady eyes taking in Celine's face. "What's wrong?" she said. "Besides being stuck down here."

"Oh, Winnie," Celine said. "I think I've done something terrible. My uncle wasn't angry to see me back. He's using me as bait."

And she poured the whole story out to Winnie's sympathetic, if sometimes itchy, ears. The petite wombat listened attentively between scratching her ears with her hind feet and her nose with the fore.

When it was over they sat in sympathetic silence, and Celine finally broke the mood by asking, "Still allergic to the leaves?"

"Yes," Winnie said, giving herself one more scratch. "But I can't stop eating."

"Did you get much before I called you down here?"

"No," Winnie answered. "Can't you hear my stomach rumbling?"

Now that she mentioned it, Celine could. She looked back up the window. No light was coming through now. She guessed it was just before dark. In her arms, Winnie started to tremble. Celine lay a comforting hand on her back.

"What is it?" she whispered.

"It's coming," Winnie said. Her voice was shaky.

For half an hour they sat, saying nothing. Celine watched the window. Winnie shook like one of the leaves she was always eating and crawled halfway under Celine's cloak.

Above, something moved in the courtyard.

The darkness in the cell grew perceptibly darker. Celine found herself beginning to tremble, but she steeled herself. Winnie kept shaking, harder now. Celine tucked the grey body all the way under her cloak and held Winnie tightly, trying to calm her down—and calm herself in the process.

Whatever it was took a long time to pass the window. A sound like rough scraping over the flagstones accompanied its movement. That, and a slow, heavy sound—breathing, Celine realized. She smelled sulfur and tried to hold her own breath.

It passed. The smell was still there. Then another sound filled the atmosphere: like a carpet beating the air. A moment later the darkness lightened again. The oppression was gone. Winnie poked her nose out of the cloak. Celine could feel the wombat's little heart beating rapidly.

On the hillside, Tomas lay next to Aldon with a dark cloak covering him from his shins to his nose. It wasn't quite long enough to cover his feet, so he'd donned a pair of dark boots and grey woolen socks that Tereska had given him. Magicked though they weren't, he hoped that a pair of feet sticking out wouldn't be too visible against the hillside. His bright hair was covered by a knit cap. His eyes peered out at the starlit sky.

Aldon, next to him, was much better covered. His shorter and stockier body was completely swathed in the dark cloak. A cap covered not only his head, but his face: only his eyes peered out, through holes Tereska had hacked in it. She had pinned the cloak around Aldon and given him strict instructions regarding his behaviour and appearance. It seemed, Tomas thought with some amusement, that she regarded Aldon as the more indispensable to her cause.

Brig, the collie, had been locked up at Tereska's apartment with much whining and protest. Tomas had to admit that he admired the ragtag duo and their dog. They were up against impossible odds, yet their faith in themselves and each other was strong enough to try anyway. They'd detailed their plans to Tomas, who privately felt they would never work but hadn't told them so. He'd face Umbria himself soon enough, and that—while it might not come out as he hoped—would certainly change everything.

A cold, barely there wind swept over the hillside, stirring the grasses. It was very quiet. The stars and moon shone down from above. The village lights were hidden by the twisting ridges and little forests, so the only other light came from the palace. Torches shone along its walls. Lights flickered in some of its windows. There were clouds over the palace, though the rest of the sky was clear, and the lights reflected off them like rust.

The wind stirred again. The dark cloaks were particularly warm and cozy. Tomas had a dreadful urge to go to sleep under his, enjoying the stars and the fresh air; to camp like a little boy.

A bell tinkled.

Beside him, Tomas heard Aldon shift. The bell tinkled again, from somewhere on the hill above them. Tomas heard hooves in the grass and the sound of something chewing. A sheep? Aldon settled back into place. The sound of the animal on the hillside only made everything more peaceful.

But then the wind changed. Something tainted the fresh air. Tomas smelled sulfur. His skin crawled as the sound of wings beating reached him, and then something huge and black came between them and the stars, and the hillside was plunged into darkness.

The creature was flying high. Tomas made out the shape of batlike wings and a long neck. Then the red eyes fixed themselves on them, and the creature dove toward the hillside.

Aldon tensed as though he would jump up and run. Tomas reached out and gripped the shepherd's arm with a hold of iron. Aldon was cold with fear. The darkness rushed all around them. The smell of sulfur and smoke filled their nostrils and throats, threatening to choke them. It was close enough to reach out and grab them . . .

And then the neck stretched out and jaws snapped shut on a sheep higher on the hillside, and the dark shape lifted up again with the hapless animal and swooped down over the crest of the ridge. Moments later the darkness began to clear and the wind to blow fresh again. Tomas let out the breath he didn't know he'd been holding. Beside him, Aldon squeaked.

"Are you all right?" Tomas whispered.

Aldon squeaked again. He cleared his throat and said, "Brig would've gotten us killed. Fool dog can't abide to let a sheep be stolen."

"Was that one of your sheep?" Tomas asked.

"Shouldn't ha' been," Aldon answered. "But I don't know why some other man's sheep would be on this hill. Especially now—that dark thing has had the whole village quaking in its nightgowns since it first appeared."

Tomas carefully folded up the dark cloak that had covered him and stood. He looked up to the top of the ridge, but all was still. "When did it first appear?" he asked.

"Two weeks tomorrow," Aldon told him. "The first night it killed fifteen kine and drove a man mad with fear." His wheat-coloured eyes looked intently through the dark at Tomas. "I couldn't make out the shape of it," he said. "Is that all the word I can bring back to Tereska—or did ye see it?"

"I saw it," Tomas said. "Not much more clearly than you did."

"But ye know what it was," Aldon said.

"Yes," Tomas said. He was almost reluctant to name it. "It was a dragon."

Chapter 8

UNWILLING TO SPEND THE REST OF THE NIGHT on the hillside but equally unwilling to chance encountering the dragon on the road, Aldon and Tomas cloaked themselves in the dark cloaks and slept in the woods. The cloaks kept them marvelously warm, and they slept well. The faint smell and pressing heaviness of the dragon's passing overhead woke them while it was still dark, but they stayed in the woods until the sun began to come up and then made their way down the narrow street of the village to Tereska's home.

Brig barked up a storm as they approached, and Tereska opened the door for them just as their feet touched the top step. Her face was drawn and pale. It was obvious she hadn't slept all night.

The smell of coffee and boiling oats struck them as soon

as they entered. Tomas pulled off his oversized boots and sat in a rickety chair. Tereska plunked a mug of bitter coffee on a little table beside him without a word, then pushed Aldon away from the stove, where he was hovering over the food.

"Fold up the dark cloaks and put them away," she told him. "Breakfast will be ready in a minute."

Aldon obeyed. He seated himself on the floor, and Brig climbed halfway into his lap, wagging his faithful tail and looking up at his master's face with his beautiful green eyes. Tomas smiled at the sight of them.

"You're always smiling," Tereska said, shoving a bowl of oatmeal into his hands. It sounded like a rebuke. "You'd think you'd be too worried to smile."

She put her hands on her hips and watched the two men as they started to eat. "Well?" she said. "What was it?"

Tomas and Aldon looked at one another. Tomas licked his lips and said, "It was a dragon."

She nodded. She seemed almost to expect it, and yet he saw the extra weariness that came into her sharp features at the words. "Should have known he'd do something like that," Tereska said. "Couldn't settle for pyrolines and plant-men, oh no."

She reached into a pocket sewn into her rags and pulled out a rolled-up piece of paper.

"Here," she told Tomas. "It's a map. I drew it all night. Tells you all I can about the palace."

She brought it down like a hammer and held it out to him. He took it, unrolling it slowly. The map was drawn in smudgy charcoal, marked here and there with drops of white wax and red splotches from a second candle. It sketched each floor of the palace out in detail, except for the dungeon and parts of the east wing. Some of its features were numbered, corresponding with notes written all down the side of the paper in tall, slanting handwriting.

"Thank you," Tomas said, looking up at her. She was still standing there, watching him through the oatmeal steam with her bony hands on her hips. One of her eyebrows was snarled in a sort of frown.

"When are you going in?" she asked.

He looked back down at the yellow paper. He sighed. "Soon."

"Celine's not a bad sort," Tereska said. Tomas looked up at her with surprise. "Not that I knew her," she hastened to explain. "But I liked her. She gave her uncle what for. Even as a child she had a lot of spunk."

Tomas tried to smile, but the detail-less space on the map, the lower floor that was the dungeon, haunted him. He kept seeing the image of the plant-men dragging Celine away.

He wondered if the memory would hurt so badly if he didn't know it was all his fault.

Once in the palace there had been a little golden-headed child named Winifred. She was the nursemaid's daughter. She was sweet and loving, and she had big blue eyes and a penchant for being in the wrong place at the wrong time. She was Celine's friend. Winifred and Celine grew up alongside each other. They were not—exactly—supposed to be friends. Celine's mother was a genteel, open-minded woman, but she was also very blue-blooded, and nursemaid's daughters were not. But they spent a fair amount of time around each other. As Winifred grew older, she became very handy with a needle and spent much of her time fixing Celine's hems and sleeves. When Celine's mother died, it was Winnie who made her grave clothes and shed tears over the headstone long after everyone else had ceased to think of it.

Ignus Umbria took no notice whatsoever of Winifred. If he knew of her existence he didn't admit to it. He was as usual embroiled in his experiments, particularly experiments that showed him how to make one thing out of another thing, no matter how unalike they were to begin with.

One day Winnie's talent for being underfoot manifested itself under Umbria's feet. He was blowing through the castle in high dudgeon, hooting and shouting to Celine about a breakthrough he'd just made in turning certain warm-blooded things into other warm-blooded things. He tripped over Winifred, picked himself up without much grace, and turned her into a wombat.

Since then, Winnie's life had a great deal more than it used to do with roots and bark, roaming in the twilight and sleeping during the day, burrowing, and instincts that buzzed and tingled and made her tremble. She kept out of the way of the pyrolines, which had spotted her once or twice and looked unnervingly eager to eat her. But she still went back to Celine's mother's headstone and cried at it sometimes.

Celine watched Winnie as she snuffled in her sleep, her large flat nose between her grey paws. She stroked the bristly fur on her friend's back and sighed to herself. She wondered now why her uncle hadn't turned her into anything. Goodness knows he'd performed enough experiments on everything else. But Celine had always thought of herself as sacred. Being sent to the moon shook that perception a little, but she'd never really thought it was forever—and she hadn't entertained the idea that her uncle wouldn't take her back. He had to. This was her home.

Ignus Umbria, the Immortal. She wondered how long he had lived. How long he had been the family's evil uncle. He hadn't always ruled the palace—far from it. In the days when Celine's father was still alive, Umbria was nothing more than an eccentric holed up in a tower, his presence tolerated because of his family connections to the queen. But then Celine's father had died in old age, leaving his much younger wife and daughter behind. Umbria came out of his tower. His experiments started to spill over. His water experiments wrecked the once-flowing fountain—it never did anything but sporadically and violently gush after he tampered with it. His uses of Ravening Fire burned a few things into oblivion. But he helped—he really did. He helped Celine's mother keep her lands and business affairs in order.

After she died, Ignus Umbria and Celine lived the tight-rope existence of two people who have known each other since the day one of them first breathed, who both lay claim to the same authority, and who both possess strong wills and quick tempers. Celine didn't try to control him or even to keep him contained. She was content to assert her own independence whenever she could, even after she'd been demoted and could prove her point only by hurling scrub brushes.

This, Celine thought bitterly, this imprisonment, was entirely against the unspoken rules. It made her angrier than his sending away of her beloved doll; angrier than his allowing the pyrolines to roam the courts without regard to her safety; angrier even than the day he turned Winnie into a wombat. That had not been fair, but neither had it been particularly premeditated.

The door to her cell burst open. Umbria stood in the open doorway, hands behind his back. Celine shoved the gently snoring Winnie into her skirt pocket and glared up at him.

"Why isn't he here yet?" Umbria demanded.

"Why should he be?" Celine snapped. "I told you he wasn't coming."

"That's impossible," Umbria said, shaking his fist. He started to pace, then turned and shouted, his face beet red, "He should have been here yesterday!"

"Well, that's not my fault, is it?" Celine yelled back. "I didn't ask you to try this. I told you he wouldn't come!"

Umbria breathed through his nose like an angry bull. He stared down at Celine.

"You had better bring him here," he said quietly. There was something in his voice that Celine had never heard before. It shook her. "I have been patient with you a very long time and you had better—oh, you had better—serve your purpose. If you don't I will make you very, very sorry."

Celine was speechless for a moment. Then she answered, "How dare you threaten me?"

He looked back at her. Slowly, he smiled. Then he turned away and shut the door behind him.

In Celine's pocket, Winnie grunted and turned herself over. Her company was a small comfort—but at least it was something. A long claw poked through the material in Celine's dress and scratched her leg.

"Ow," Celine said to herself. Then she paused in mid-pain. With a sudden burst of energy she shook Winifred out of her pocket.

"Winnie!" she whispered. "Wake up!" The miniature wombat curled up into a ball on the floor and continued to snore. Celine poked her. "Wake up!"

With an unhappy snuffling sound, Winnie uncurled herself, scratched at the air, and blinked up at Celine, who was bent over her with an unwontedly animated expression.

"Too much light," Winnie mumbled.

Celine glanced up at the scant light coming in the window. Bother whatever whim of her uncle's had made Winifred nocturnal. Of course, that same whim had given her impressive claws and nearly tireless energy at night, when she was driven by hunger and an instinct to dig.

"How big a tunnel can you dig?" Celine asked.

Winnie squinted at her. She had wrinkled her entire snout in protest against the sun. "Dunno," she said. "Big enough for you."

Celine sat back with a triumphant smile. A moment later she scooped Winnie up and tucked her back into her skirt, still smiling as the furry creature's breathing grew deep and regular again.

"Perfect," Celine said.

A lone dark figure trekked over the Fallow Fields of Brusa by night. Whatever ghosts haunted those plains, they did not bother him. He crept into Meru early one morning, took himself to a tavern, and began to listen. His search was at first unfruitful. No one had a word to say about the golden Immortal or the beautiful woman he'd had with him. For a while he feared they had not come to Meru . . . but no. Where else would they have gone?

He lessened his caution. He asked questions. Still, no one gave him the information he wanted. Then one night he stood on the docks and looked up at the high clock tower, and he saw a figure standing on the other side of the glass beneath the giant minute hand. The figure was visible because of a candle in his hand. The figure, moreover, was familiar.

He made several attempts to gain entrance to the clock tower and failed. At last he threw caution to the wind and started to climb up the locks and chains. So it was that he found a sort of staircase carved into the side, one that led to a little door high in the wall.

And so it was that when Grandfather Monk opened his eyes to greet the sunrise in the morning, he found himself looking into the face of Malic.

"You!" Grandfather Monk gasped, struggling to sit up against the weight that always seemed to push down on him. "What are you doing here?"

"Yes, it's me," Malic said. "I've found you at last, old fool. Where are they?"

Grandfather Monk blinked. Into his still befuddled mind came the understanding that Malic was looking for Tomas and Celine. He felt something warm and furry at his ankles. The pyroline. It stared out at Malic with unblinking eyes. Malic looked down at it a moment, but his expression was contemptuous. Then he stood from the stool where he'd perched himself and took a step toward Monk, his fist clenched and half-raised.

"Tell me!" he said. "Where have they gone?"

Grandfather Monk held up his dignified head. "I'll not tell you," he said.

Malic grabbed the old man's shirt collar with both hands and hauled him half out of his seat. "That's what you think!" he said.

At that moment the pyroline sprang into action, hissing and squalling like a teakettle gone mad, tiny wisps of smoke rising from its grey-tufted orange ears. Malic dropped Monk and jumped back, startled. "What is that?" he demanded.

Grandfather Monk put his hands on the bench where he'd been sleeping and pushed himself onto his shaky legs. "I'll not tell you a thing," he said in a tremulous voice. A broom leaned against a shelf near him, and he took this up and brandished it. "Be gone, wicked one!"

Malic growled. He drew his fist back, but thought better of attacking Monk. The man was so old that a single blow would likely silence him forever, and then the trail would be colder than it had been even in the streets below.

Malic held up his hands as though in surrender. "Easy now, old man," he said. "I mean no harm."

"Then be off with you!" Monk said, thrusting the broom handle forward.

Malic cast his eyes about the strange quarters with its eclectic collection of artifacts for something to help him deal with the unexpectedly resistant old man. He had long ago forgotten that Monk had anything in him that needed dealing with. The old fellow had allowed himself to be deceived and used without much fuss, but Tomas's reappearance after ninety-three years seemed to have galvanized him into quite a different sort of man.

His eyes fell on a map, stretched across a wooden frame, with sketches of strange monsters and warnings painted in its corners. The map showed long stretches of sea, with small islands and large, and in the north, a wide land with a palace sketched in disproportionate size and detail. Faced with such a large number of possible places to go, the scheming mind of Malic realized that it did not matter if Monk never voluntarily told him where Tomas was. He could be tricked into revealing it.

Malic smiled. He turned away from Monk with his broomstick and the still-bristling pyroline as though they were not really worth his notice. He stalked across the wooden floor to the map and jabbed a thick finger at it—not specifically at any part of it, but with enough purpose and force to make it look as though he had.

"Just as I thought," he said. He bowed to Grandfather Monk with a small smile. "You've given it away."

Grandfather Monk turned pale. The broomstick shook in his old hands. "No!" he said.

Malic's face turned dark and frightening. "I know where they are," he said in a low voice. "I'm going to find them now, and when I do, I'll make them sorry they ever breathed. Did you see how they treated me? Oh, you did, I know you did. Watch if I don't give the same to them. I'll put that god of yours in the stocks till his hair falls out, and stab the girl so full of needle-holes she won't dare breathe for fear of her breath escaping out them."

The broomstick was shaking so badly now that its straw

end rattled the shelf next to Monk. "You won't," the old man said. The old note of misery was back in his voice. His faith in Tomas and Celine was shaken by his long-time fear and bondage to Malic. He had seen Malic do many terrible things and defeat very many people. He had only seen Tomas win one battle—and how much of a victory had that been, if the man was standing here now, threatening to track him down?

But . . . but . . . Monk's faith fought for the upper hand. Had he not seen Celine behaving like a queen? Had he not seen Tomas vanish after her by magic, like a hero of old, off to rescue his lady? Were they not even now defeating the enemy who had threatened her? And would they not do it again?

They would, they would. Monk knew they would. Hope burst out of him in words. "They'll show you!" he said.

Malic turned back to him with his dark eyes glinting. "Not if they don't see me coming," he said.

And then, with his words spoken and all his cunning damage done, he turned and disappeared into the shadows of the clock tower.

Grandfather Monk did not sit back down. His shaking knees would not allow him to. There were tears on his deeply wrinkled cheeks. Hope and fear wrestled within him. He needed to go to them—to find them—to warn them. He needed to play his part in this story. He had promised Tomas he would not die, but what was the point of living if there was nothing more for you to do? He had asked himself that question several times in the sea-hushed quiet of the clock tower. Now he knew. This was his something more.

Grandfather Monk was in many ways a foolish and simple man, but some wisdom still remained to him. He did not know where Tomas and Celine had gone, nor where to reach them. But how to find them he knew full well.

He stooped over as best he could, picked up the pyroline, and held it at eye level. "Where?" he asked it in trembling tones. "Where have they gone?"

The pyroline blinked at him. Then it meowed, just as if it were a usual cat and not a fire-cat with magic in its veins, and squirmed its way out of Grandfather Monk's hands. It landed neatly on the floor and held its tail in the air like a parade major's baton. It took a few steps forward, meowed again, and turned its grey-orange head to give Monk a pointed look.

He got the idea. With a shaky mix of excitement and fear, Grandfather Monk hefted the broom over his shoulder, slipped his feet into his boots, and started after the pyroline.

Malic watched from the shadows, tucked behind a pile of rusty lamp holders and a candle six inches on every side that had the colour and smell of dusky cranberry. He smiled. As he started to his feet, something above caught his eye. It was tucked into a cubbyhole, but the very tip was still protruding. It was rounded and gleaming gold—like a sword hilt.

His eyes greedy, Malic jumped high enough to grab the hilt and pull it down. A long, slender sword appeared in his hands. It was sheathed in ivory. Its blade, as he pulled it free, was silver and finely wrought. The hilt was made of gold, and it shone brightly—except for one soot-smudged place just at the base of the blade. There seemed to be writing there. Malic squinted. He carried the sword out into the light, nearly tripping over various paraphernalia in his way. As the morning light brought the words into sharp relief, Malic's eyes widened.

There were two words engraved on the hilt. They said "Umbria's Bane."

Suddenly, Malic, who had never met Ignus Umbria but had heard a great deal about him in his cruelty-loving life, had a very good idea where Monk was headed. Other ideas were springing up in his head like pernicious weeds, and they all made him smile through his thick dark beard. Ideas of alliance. Ideas of bringing his enemies to a miserable, miserable defeat.

The first step was obvious.

Give Umbria the sword.

Pyrolines were not well-loved creatures in general. They had all the vices of cats with few of their good points. They were not, as a rule, content to sit on anyone's lap and purr. They preferred to crawl into the very hot ashes left over from some terribly destructive fire and there preen themselves, and if they actually chanced to make their way into a presently blazing fire, they became something most unkittenlike—something downright terrifying. All truly great fires being, as they are, destructive, pyrolines were generally happiest when other people were still stammering in shock over their loss of home, wealth, or life.

So it was not entirely the usual thing that Tomas should find and adopt a pyroline kit, or that it should adopt him back. But Tomas often did unusual things, and this pyroline was not particularly a paragon of its kind. It was smaller than the usual run of pyrolines, less vicious, and really more friendly to people—and other creatures.

The pyroline was a very tiny kit when Tomas found it. It was the runt of its litter, and its mother had abandoned it to follow a circus with a man who played with fire. The other kits tried to eat it, in a manner not unlike pyrolines. The kit managed to get away, but it was hurt in the process, and only a kind miller who gave it a lit oil lamp stood between it and death.

Then Tomas disappeared, and did not come back for ninety-three years.

A well-fed pyroline could last a very long time, as creatures of magic generally could, but the orange-and-grey kit was not a favourite for lasting. He was still too small and too passive. He did not just give up, though. He traveled the highways and byways of the world, mewling at doors for candles and lamps and bits of cooking coal. And then he reached the sea, where a most extraordinary thing happened.

He saw a star fall into the water while it was still burning. The star exploded with the brightest flame in the world, even though it was in the water. The pyroline, going against the way of all cats in the world, threw itself into the water and swam toward the flame.

He reached it. The fire burned, down below the water, for a year and three days. And for that year and three days, the little pyroline was the happiest creature in the world.

The story didn't end there, though. For stars are not simply creatures of flame. They are also creatures of spirit, and when they fall their spirits blow out into the world and become contrary winds—the sort of winds that blow sailors off course and cause fires to grow; winds that carry voices with messages and send storms into strange places. The sort of winds that have minds of their own and behave very much as though they do not belong to the normal run of things at all. Which, of course, they don't.

This particular star-spirit became a mistral . . . and not just a mistral, but a magistral. This was not merely a playful breeze. It was a wind with purpose and design and wisdom, for it had once been the spirit of a very great star.

The magistral was waiting for the little pyroline and the old man when they reached the harbour. It was blowing in barely perceptible little puffs, roughing up the water here and there. The pyroline knew it well, and he led Grandfather Monk straight to a small skiff that was surrounded, over and under, immersed, in fact, by the unseen magistral that had been a star.

It blew Grandfather Monk's wispy strands of white hair as they approached. The old man was clutching his broomstick with great determination. His heart was beating rapidly. The descent from the clock tower had been accomplished by sheer miraculous blind fortune. The pyroline jumped into the skiff and looked at Grandfather Monk expectantly. He climbed in, narrowly avoiding a headlong pitch over the side, and seated himself with the broomstick held up like a flag. He nodded gravely to the pyroline.

"Lead on, little friend," he said.

And the magistral began to blow. It blew so cannily that it managed to unfurl the sail all on its own, for Monk had no idea how to manage a craft of any kind. It carefully maneuvered the skiff through the harbour, past the tall ships and waiting fisherboats, into the great open water.

And then it truly began to blow. The magistral unleashed all the grand power of its ancient spirit and drove the skiff straight across the sea to the land where Umbria's palace lay. The little pyroline sat in the prow with its orange-grey tufts flying and its eyes drinking in the sea.

Behind them came another little boat. No one saw it. Even the magistral, lost in its own magnificent fury of power and sound, did not notice what it was dragging in its wake. Malic's going was not so smooth, but he knew how to sail, and his own powerful drive—that of revenge—kept him alert and strong. He caught the tail of the magistral's work and flew across the sea in the wake of his duped leader.

Ignus Umbria stood in one of the highest towers of the palace with his hands clasped behind his back, looking out to sea.

The sea was not actually visible from the palace. Until she visited Meru with Tomas, Celine had never seen it. But Umbria's eyes were very good, and his imagination was better.

He had a feeling that something was coming to him over the water.

He smiled. His beautiful fingers tightened around each other. He would not have to wait much longer.

Chapter 9

LAD FOR ONCE THAT THERE WAS LITTLE LIGHT coming through the window, Celine curled up in the very center of the cell floor—a good distance away from the water-streaked walls, which had, despite her attempts to remember not to lean against them, already made her far wetter, dirtier, and colder than was comfortable—and tried to sleep. It was the middle of the day and thus sleeping did not come easily, but she closed her eyes and tried to push her way into dreamland.

Her thoughts were uncooperative. They squabbled and clucked until she took them firmly in hand, demanded they behave, and finally managed to blank out her mind.

Thoughts, even when they are quiet, leave impressions of themselves on the mind. Celine's impressions were confused. One was anxiety for the future mingled with excitement at the plan due to commence in the twilight. One was anger, still seething at her uncle. And one, perched atop the others, turning itself around and around like a gem trying to catch the sunlight, was a curious sensation she didn't know how to interpret. She felt it every time she thought of Tomas.

She hoped, of course, that Tomas wasn't coming. At exactly the same time, she hoped he was. Celine had never been in love before. Besides her uncle, the male entities around the palace were mostly green, thorny, and poison-ivy-rash inducing, so there hadn't been much opportunity. Nor did Celine consider herself especially romantic, as she had her hands full without adding such emotional nonsense to her days. She was quite certain that she was not in love now. But there was a queer, fluttery feeling in her stomach when she pictured Tomas's warm-candle eyes, and his first words to her would keep running through her head.

Bother, she realized, she was thinking again. She frowned, her eyes still closed, and commanded the thoughts to settle down. Grudgingly, they did. But they kept flashing little bits of colour at her while she tried to sleep.

She woke up stiff and sore. Winnie was buried in the length of her skirt and was evidently snuffling around in her pocket. Celine pushed herself up on her hands just as Winnie's grey snout poked up out of the pile of cloth.

"There you are," Winnie said.

"Good, you're awake," Celine said. She was foggier than she sounded. Confused thoughts were still rushing around in her head, but they more unruly now that she'd been sleeping. It seemed to her she'd been dreaming, but she couldn't remember. She took a deep breath and tried to clear her head. "Winnie," she said, "we need to get out of here." She got up, fighting off slight dizziness.

"Now?" Winnie asked. "How?"

"Now," Celine said. "But it will take a while."

"Whatever you say," Winnie said. "But dinner is calling."

"Can't you ignore it?" Celine asked.

Winnie's beady black eyes looked pathetic. "I would," she said. "But my stomach has voices and they're all clamouring."

"I'm hungry myself," Celine confessed. Her stomach grumbled in assent. Her uncle hadn't fed her since throwing her in here. The water running down the walls was convenient for staying hydrated, but it lacked any substantial nutrition. Maybe, Celine reflected, that was why she was so dizzy.

"Just talk with me for a few minutes," Celine said. "Then you can go and eat. Quickly. And come back."

"What do you need to know?" Winnie asked.

"I want us to get out of here," Celine said.

"You said that."

"Yes, I know. I was thinking about how to do it, and I can only see one way."

Winnie looked up at the high window and then down at the barred door. "I don't see any way."

Here Celine looked proud of herself. "We'll dig our way out," she announced.

Winnie's ear twitched. She scratched it fiercely. "We?" she said.

"Well," Celine said. "You'll have to start."

Winnie looked around, moving her front paws and following with her head, until she'd turned herself in a full circle. "This whole floor is stone," she said. "I can't dig through stone."

"Don't worry about that," Celine said. "Just tell me again that you can dig a tunnel big enough for me to fit through."

Winnie blinked up at her a moment, scratched again, and said, "Of course. You should see some of my burrows."

"You're going to have to do it quickly," Celine said. "It's a good thing my uncle isn't making a habit of . . . oh, Winnie, you're shaking."

The wombat was still sitting in one place on the stone floor, but she was trembling from her claws to the tips of her ears. Her eyes were still pathetic. "I'm hungry," she explained. Celine realized that her friend was holding herself in place, determinedly not hunting down dinner.

"Get going, then," Celine said. She scooped Winnie up and boosted her up to a few rough stones below the window. The petite wombat scrambled the rest of the way up, turned to look down at Celine with an unintelligible wombat expression, and disappeared.

"Hurry back," Celine said.

The cell had suddenly become lonelier. Fighting off a sense of desolation, Celine knelt and began to run her fingers along the cracks in the flagstones.

She was looking for weak places in the floor. She was sure they had to be there, for several reasons. First, among her very few and very dim memories of her father was one of him ranting about the poor construction of the palace where they lived. Her family's opinion of peasants had never been very high, and peasants had built this place. Even more promising was the water running down the walls. Magic, strong though it was in itself, had a way of weakening ordinary things that it came into contact with. This meant that Umbria, in magicking the dungeon with dampness to make it more suitably dungeonlike, had made the actual stone weaker than it should have been. He could have magicked the stone too, of course. But Celine was quite certain he hadn't.

Her fingers found a particular deep and wide crack in the floor, and she dug her fingertips into the earth between its sides. With a great deal of digging and scratching, she managed to clear out enough of the earth to reach the bottom of the flagstone. She curled her fingers under the edge, got off her knees and onto her feet to give herself more leverage, and pulled with all her might.

The stone didn't move.

Gasping, Celine gave herself a rest. Then she took a deep breath and tried again, throwing all of her strength—and more, her will—into the effort. This time it budged.

For the next forty minutes Celine strained and pulled.

She got on her back and pushed with her feet, got on her knees and heaved with her shoulder, and finally—after bruising, scraping, and battering herself, and with a few impressive tears in her clothes—the stone came out of the floor completely and fell to one side. In its place was a square of dark, damp, compressed earth, roughly three feet by three feet, totally void of roots or grubs or any of the other things sometimes found under slabs of stone.

Celine leaned against the wall. She let the water run into her hair and down the back of her dress, cooling her off. She swallowed and fought for air. Her heart was pounding, and she was proud.

But forty minutes had passed, and Winnie had not returned.

In the courtyard above, Winifred in wombat form was eagerly biting and gnawing her way through the chestnut bush in one of the gardens. She had reached the very center of an especially thick shrubbery. Crickets jumped away from her claws as she pushed even further. Intent on keeping Celine company, she had gone far longer than usual without eating. The girl inside was concerned only with faithfulness; the wombat outside was ravenous. For an hour at least, the girl was forced to succumb to the twin demands of hunger and instinctual drive.

The drive was strong tonight. The need to consume

rang in Winnie's ears, overcoming even the allergic itch that demanded she pay attention to it, and kept her moving forward . . . forward . . .

Until she spilled out of the chestnut bushes altogether and found herself completely exposed on the flagstones. It took her a moment to realize what had happened. But before she could turn around and bury herself once more in the shrubbery, something reached down and picked her up.

Winnie looked up, terrified, into the inhuman face of one of the plant-men. Its fingers around her were tight enough to constrict her breath. The plant-man's dull eyes looked her over curiously, and it turned her upside down and shook her. Bits of leaf and bark rained out of her fur.

The plant-man frowned. He looked past Winnie to the chestnut bush and the clear damage that had been done to it. He looked back down at his captive. The expression on his face, not very subtle, turned from one of curiosity to one of enmity.

Winnie began to kick and squirm, but the terrible fingers held tight.

Tomas stood on the ridge in the evening light and looked down at the palace. He wore a new pair of oversized boots and a cloak, sans holes, that Tereska had given him. Other than that, he was dressed just as he had been for the last ninety-three years. The holes in his shirt which Celine had tried to sew up before being interrupted by Malic and Grandfather Monk were still there.

He looked something like a hobo in need of work, or perhaps like a hero home from a long, long war. A glorious hero or hobo, because Tomas was always glorious if one looked at him twice. His hair was golden and splendid; his face was strong and handsome in the purple twilight. And today, it was preoccupied.

Many visions attempted to attach themselves to his view of the palace. Visions of Celine suffering untold hardship in the dungeon—probably languishing, Tomas thought, as beautifully as she had done on the moon. But in the dungeon she was truly alone, as she had not been in the heavens, where Tomas, unbeknownst to her, had been watching—and watching over her. Visions of the great black dragon. Visions of men made of rosebushes patrolling the walls. These last two did not bother him much. There were not many things in the world that Tomas was afraid to face.

The most persistent vision was different. It was a vision of a small man with a long face, sharp eyes, and beautiful fingers. An artist, a scientist, a magician—and the reason for Tomas's existence. Ignus Umbria, with whom Tomas must one day meet. Ignus Umbria, who had inspired in Tomas's life several hundred years of procrastination.

Celine had brought everything to a head. Tomas cared what happened to her, and so he could not go on pretending that a man existed who could destroy him, and whom he could likewise destroy—whom he must, in fact, destroy.

Tomas began to sidle down the ridge. If it had not been so steep his walk could have been called a stride, but even Immortals must beware lest they trip. He whistled to himself as he went.

Under the circumstances, it was a very strange thing to do. But Tomas had never been much like other men.

He whistled all the way down the ridge, through the long, waving grasses at the bottom, and up the stone road to the palace gates. He raised his fist to knock. Simultaneously, he ceased to whistle.

One, two, three times he knocked. His knuckles made a dull sound on the thick door. He stood back and waited for someone to open.

No one did.

Tomas sighed, stepped forward, and knocked again. It really was a very dull sound, that of his fist on the wood. A dull, quiet sound. There was no knocker—no conceivable way of making more noise. The villagers, Tomas realized, were not exactly encouraged to visit this place. No wonder Aldon wanted to wrest control of the lands away from Umbria entirely.

Aldon and Tereska had no idea Tomas was here. None at all. He hadn't told them. He had simply told them he was going for a stroll, which he was—straight to the house of Umbria.

Once more Tomas went up to the door and knocked. This time he pounded with all his might, and kicked once for good measure. His efforts were met by a loud squawk.

A large, clumsy white bird sailed over the top of the gates, circled around squawking a few times, and settled itself on the top of the doors. It looked down at Tomas with remarkably intelligent eyes, and then it barked.

Tomas blinked. From its goony efforts at landing, Tomas suspected this was the bird through whose eyes he had seen the courtyard—the bird that had witnessed Celine being dragged away. Still, he had not expected it to bark at him. Encouraged that at least someone was paying attention, Tomas hauled back and kicked the door again. He was grateful for Tereska's boots. Without them his toes would have been bruised by now, and less noisy besides.

The plant-man holding Winnie looked up at the sound of barking. It frowned and looked back at its struggling captive. Its fingers had tightened around her, and she was fighting for breath now.

The bird over the gates took off again, making such a racket that it could not ignored any longer. Without a sound, the plant-man dropped Winnie on the floor of the courtyard and strode to join one of its fellows at the gate.

Winifred lay on the hard pavement, gasping and panting. She was twitching with fright, but her hunger was gone. As soon as she could master herself, she scrambled to her feet and dashed for the dungeon aperture and the safety of Celine.

The bird flapped back into the air and circled around, squawking, diving, and once again barking. It only managed to get one or two of these incongruous noises out, but they were enough. On the rampart of the wall, two heads suddenly appeared. They were green, leafy, and inhuman. They stared down at Tomas without a word.

"I want to see Ignus Umbria," he called up, as though he were a new neighbour requesting a cup of sugar.

The heads disappeared. Ten minutes later, the gates began to slowly creak their way open. They opened to a spacious, beautifully manicured courtyard. A few lamps had been lit, casting shadows over the pale stones. Gardens rustled in a soft breeze.

Before this pleasant vista stood four men made of vegetable matter. Their arms, hands, and fingers looked like thick, woody vines twisted together. Their legs might have been the same, but they weren't visible beneath purple livery and knee-high leather boots. Their heads, which included the usual humanoid features of eyes, nose, mouth, and ears and yet lacked any spark of personality—the latent deadness of their eyes was in itself somehow menacing—were large and rather more like big green cabbage roses than any truly human head.

Their appearance might have startled Tomas very badly, except that he had seen them through the looking glass once already and was, furthermore, not usually startled. It is a characteristic of Immortality to take things more or less in stride.

The plant-men did not speak. Instead, they formed themselves in a rectangle around Tomas and began to march. He went along with them. They took him across the stones of the courtyard and through a high pair of yellow doors. This led into a wide and tastefully decorated corridor, padded with oriental carpets, paste busts and paintings and a great harp.

They stopped in front of a very large painting of the night sky over a forest. Tomas was admiring it when the plant-men opened a door and ushered him through it. He went, leaving the plant-men in the hallway. The room which he entered was small. It had a fireplace and two plushly cushioned chairs. It had no windows or other doors.

He was still observing this when the door behind him slammed shut, and he heard a key turn in the lock.

Winnie hurtled through the aperture with such force that she hardly had time to catch herself. She half-tumbled, half-climbed through the opening, lost her footing, and pitched headlong toward the elbow-deep hole in which Celine was digging. Celine heard the entrance and looked up just in time to catch Winnie in her dirt-caked arms.

"What took you?" she asked.

Winnie only shook her head. She couldn't answer. Winifred the girl had been timid, but courageous enough. Winifred the wombat tried, but instinct regularly reduced her to a trembling mass of inability. More so since Celine had come back. She stiffened herself in Celine's arms and tried valiantly to get a grip on herself.

Her recovery didn't take long. When she had ceased trembling, Celine set her down on the floor next to the hole. Winnie crawled forward and sniffed at it. It was just deep enough to cover Winnie's head if she were to jump in.

"How long have you been working on that?" she asked.

"An hour and a half," Celine said. "Ever since you left."

Winnie scratched her ear. "It's not bad. A little amateurish."

"Forgive me," Celine said. "I don't burrow often."

Winnie made a chuckling sound which Celine assumed was wombat laughter. "Apparently," she said. She crawled forward, tumbled into the hole, and started digging. Her strong legs, wide paws, and long claws did their work well. Dirt flew everywhere, clods of it hitting Celine's dress or the floor with a soft thump. The hole began to widen almost immediately. Winnie was a blur of efficiency—a veritable virtuoso of digging.

"Bravo," Celine said with a grin. "Can I help?"

Winnie shook her head. Her reply was muffled, as her nose was in the bottom of the swiftly deepening space.

"Clean up," she said.

Celine looked around her. The dirt was piling up fast. Winnie was right—if she didn't do something with it, it would soon start sliding back into the hole. She looked down at her hands, dirt in every knuckle and under every fingernail. She was smeared with mud up to her elbows and streaked even beyond that, and her clothes—beautiful clothes—were filthy. She sighed a little but wasted no more time in getting on her knees and shoving the dirt back. As there were no brooms or shovels in reach, she could do just as well as Winnie and use her own two hands.

Ignus Umbria entered the room with a flourish. Tomas was sitting in the nicer of the plush chairs, leaning toward the fireplace with his elbows on his knees. He looked up at Ignus's entry, his eyes mildly surprised.

Umbria looked his adversary up and down and sneered.

"Did you make those boots?" he asked.

"No," Tomas told him.

"It's about time you arrived," Umbria said. He did not cackle, but his words had a cackling tone nonetheless.

"Listen," Tomas said. "I'm here to make you a deal. I don't really want to destroy you."

"Of course you don't," Umbria said.

"So just let me take Celine away," Tomas said, "and I'll

go away and leave you alone for another hundred years."

Umbria laughed in Tomas's face. It was a harsh laugh, lacking its usual unhinged enthusiasm and glee. "Do you suppose I'm going to let you dictate the terms?"

Tomas folded his hands pleasantly. "Why not?" he asked.

"There are other options," Umbria said. "Other possibilities you seem to have overlooked."

Tomas blinked. "I confess, I don't see them."

Umbria turned red. "There is the possibility that I could destroy you."

"Oh," Tomas said. "I suppose so. But it's not very likely, is it? At the very least you would be taking a chance. Now, you don't want me to be here, and neither do I. Will you let me see Celine?" He stood as he spoke. His lanky height made Umbria look like a particularly squat spider in the presence of a young and golden grasshopper.

Umbria's long face had gone from red to purple, but he made not a sound through the spectrum. He looked up at Tomas now and said, "You shall see her, yes. And then, my young friend, we will sit down and discuss the real options."

He turned stiffly around and walked through the door. He held it open and motioned for Tomas to pass through with exaggerated courtesy. A nasty light was dancing in his eyes.

In the dungeon, the tunnel was coming along faster than Celine had imagined it could. The hole was five feet down now and just wide enough for Celine to move inside, and she had climbed into it to scoop loose dirt out and shove it away from the hole's edges as fast as Winnie sent it out. Winnie didn't bother to aim, so Celine had dirt in her mouth and eyes and down the collar of her dress, but she was exhilarated.

Five feet six inches down, Winnie suddenly switched directions and began to dig sideways. This tunnel was low and wide, and Celine could already see that she would have to go through it on her belly. She considered protesting but decided against it. If Winnie could live half her life underground, Celine could bear it for the length of time it took to escape the dungeon. Winnie was angling down as she dug, and though the angle wasn't steep, Celine thought between handfuls of dirt that she'd be grateful when the tunnel began to head up.

From inside the tunnel, Winnie said something. Celine dropped to her knees, stuck her head into the darkness, and said, "What?"

"Get in here," Winnie said. "Pack the dirt in after us."

"We'll be trapped," Celine said.

Winnie turned around and gave her a beady-eyed look. "We'll be safe," she said.

Celine crawled forward. Winnie had widened the tunnel more than she thought—she could crawl on her elbows, though not on her knees. "I need more room," she said.

"All right," Winnie said. "Just stay close to me. Use your feet to pack the dirt if you can."

Celine began to obey. Her stomach was queasy as she worked. "Winnie," she said, "where are we going?"

"To my great burrow," Winnie said. "And then out."

Umbria hurried Tomas through the halls with the air of an excited conqueror. He talked as they went, urging him to come faster.

"You'll see her," he said. "Very comfortable, she is. Right at home!" He cackled. "You'll be most pleased to see how comfortable she is, and how little difference you can make for her!"

Tomas stopped suddenly. Umbria almost tripped over his own feet.

"Why have you stopped?" he shrieked.

Tomas spoke calmly, without any sign of emotion on his face. "I will make a difference for her," he said. "And if I find that you've treated her very badly, you will feel the consequences of it."

In reply Umbria only cackled again. He took Tomas's arm and nearly shoved him forward. "Come along, come along," he said.

They rushed through increasingly narrow, twisting corridors, and then down a shallow flight of steps. At the base of these they came into a guards' floor full of open rooms where guards no longer dwelt. The plant-men stayed here, as was evident by the bits of dry foliage on the floor and caught in spiderwebs, but nothing human had been here for years.

Here Umbria unlocked a heavy wooden door festooned with iron spikes. He swung it open. Another set of stairs plunged down into a dark, wet dungeon. Water was running down the wall of the stairwell but not, curiously, collecting on the floor. Umbria touched the walls as they descended the steps.

"Good and wet," he said. "Nothing like damp to make a dungeon, eh? That's what I've always read."

The dungeon was lit only very faintly, by a phosphorescent lichen that grew along the wall in places. Tomas looked up and thought he could see narrow windows letting in moonlight, but he wasn't certain—it was too dark. Umbria found a torch and lit it. A few paces into the dungeon, he stopped before a barred door and waved his hand triumphantly.

"There you are, my young friend!" he announced loudly. "What do you say to that?"

Tomas peered through the bars, and his golden eyebrows rose. A smile began to play on his face. He straightened up and looked at Umbria. "There's no one there," he said.

Umbria blinked. He spun on his heel and peered through.

The cell looked as though some disaster had hit it. One of its paving stones lay atop the floor, and all around it dirt was piled in heaps, clumps, and hills. A gaping dark spot at the center of this suggested a hole.

Umbria fumbled for his keys. He pulled one out and unlocked the door, then barged in with his torch held high. It was indeed a hole—just wide enough for a human to fit down it. It went straight down for about five feet, and then it changed directions and became a tunnel. Umbria knelt down, holding his torch low so he could see. A wall of dirt met his gaze just inside the tunnel.

He cursed. He cursed again, more loudly. He stood and shouted, "Guards!"

Then he rounded on Tomas with a look of wild fury and shouted, "Where is she?"

Chapter 10

ELINE STOPPED PACKING DIRT BEHIND HER and leaned forward on her elbows. Her legs were cramped and aching. Her neck hurt—her head felt as though it weighed fifty pounds. Her shoulders hurt from carrying all that weight, and she was sick to death of the darkness and lack of air.

"Winnie," she said. Her voice came out in a croak.

The wombat stopped digging for a moment. "What?" she asked.

"Did you hear something?" Celine asked.

They both fell silent. A distant sound reached their ears—a sound from behind them.

"Yes," Winnie said. Her ear twitched, and she reached up and scratched it with her back foot.

"My uncle," Celine said. "He found it." She pulled herself ahead on her elbows, shoving dirt back and kicking it into place. "Go faster, Winnie!"

Winnie obeyed. She pointed her nose downward and began to dig faster than ever. Celine closed her eyes against the spray of damp earth and moved forward blindly.

She heard the scrape of claws against something hard.

"Oh, no!" Winnie squeaked.

"What is it?" Celine asked. She kept her eyes closed.

"I think it's the foundation," Winnie said. "But it shouldn't be here . . . I thought . . ." She kept scratching. She couldn't angle downward anymore, so her little tunnel moved straight ahead as she clawed at the stone below her.

It wasn't the foundation. It was a roof. Winnie discovered this a minute later, when her claws uncovered a hole in it and she fell through.

Celine heard a squeak and the sound of rushing air. A peculiar and unpleasant smell tickled her nose. She reached out for Winnie but found nothing but dirt and air. She opened her eyes. A faint orange light was coming up from a hole in the floor of the tunnel.

Celine wriggled forward and looked through the hole.

The morning Tomas was born, in a little thatched-roof

stone cottage, a stork landed on the chimney and dropped something down it. That's how they knew he was Immortal. Immortals always came with at least one accessory. It was that object which was meant to set the course of their lives.

Tomas's was a sword with the words *Umbria's Bane* on it.

No one was especially happy about this, least of all Tomas's mother, and later, as he grew older, least of all Tomas. When a sword was delivered to one at birth with a very specific purpose, it indicated that one's future would be violent and disturbing. Tomas was not, as a child, any more given to violence and disturbance than he was as a man. He preferred to make beautiful and useful things, and to smile and kiss his mother's cheek whenever possible.

For the first twenty-five years of his long life Tomas ignored the sword. His mother had wrapped it in linen and shoved it into a corner of the attic so Tomas wouldn't hurt himself with it as a boy, and there he was happy to leave it.

Around that time he first heard of Umbria. Umbria was also Immortal, a bit older than Tomas. Just what his purpose was Tomas could not ascertain, try though he might to puzzle it out. But it was clear from the stories about the man that he was brilliant—and far more given to violence and disturbance than Tomas would ever be. In fact, it became clear that someday someone would have to stop him.

As *Umbria's Bane* was reclining in his attic, Tomas was the obvious candidate.

But his mother was old, his father was ailing, and Umbria was not always awful. He had calm periods. Long times in which no word of him reached Tomas. More years passed in which Tomas did not go out to fulfill his destiny. Then his parents died in short succession, and on a golden day Tomas went up under the thatch, brushed away the cobwebs, and pulled *Umbria's Bane* out of the linen.

Sword in hand, he began to trek across the world in search of Umbria. As he went, he learned to fight. He saw battles and even participated in one.

He hated it.

He reached a small country where Umbria had set himself up as a despot. Assuredly, he needed to be stopped. Tomas meant to stop him. But before he actually knocked on the gates of the castle where Umbria had holed himself up, he met a little girl with braids wrapped around her head and freckles on her nose, a little girl with no family who needed someone to take care of her.

And she liked Tomas, and asked if he would do it.

He hemmed and hawed, but he took her to an inn in the meantime and fed her dinner, and then acquired some new clothes for her, and started to teach her to read. All of this took about a week. While he was doing it, a peasant uprising overthrew Ignus Umbria.

And so defeating him was not *so* pressing after all.

Raising the little girl until she was grown and happily married took sixteen years, after which Tomas found more and more things to keep him busy, and finally he stuck the sword into a hole in the clock tower in Meru and waited for Umbria to become so bad, so destructive, so aggressively vile that he couldn't be ignored anymore.

He had never expected that day to touch him quite so personally. He hadn't seen Celine coming at all.

Now, as he stood looking at the hole in the floor of the dungeon, hope welled up in Tomas and he thought to himself that perhaps it had happened again. Something else had stopped Umbria, and so he didn't have to do it.

Umbria wheeled on Tomas and glared at him. "You planned this, didn't you?" he asked. "You knew she'd do something foolish. You think this has crippled me—that my playing cards are all gone."

"It does look that way," Tomas said.

"Perhaps it does," Umbria said. "But this isn't over. I'll find her yet. I'll make her pay for making a fool of me. As for you, my young friend, the time has come for you to see the place I've prepared for you."

"Actually," Tomas said, "I think it's time for me to leave."

He pulled his ring out of his pocket and slipped it on his finger, bracing for transport. He screwed his eyes shut as the cool metal slid over his skin.

Nothing happened.

Umbria began to laugh. "Let you down, has it?" he asked between laughs. "Amateurs shouldn't play with magic."

Tomas tore the ring from his finger and turned it in his hand. A terrible fear had seized him. Umbria must have seen it in his face, because he said, "No, she's not dead. But she doesn't have the ring. I do."

Tomas looked wordlessly at his adversary.

"Do you think I don't know a magic ring when I see it?" Umbria said. "I have been playing with magic since you were still playing with hobbyhorses and baby rattles. I took it off her the moment she arrived." An odd look—half smug grin, half piqued curiosity—came over his face. "I didn't realize it was a paired ring. Fascinating."

He held out his hand, palm up. "Give it to me."

Tomas slipped the ring back into his pocket. "I think I won't."

Umbria shouted so suddenly that Tomas jumped. "Guards!"

Tomas turned and saw the plant-men coming in. He knew several things. He knew that he was not stronger than the plant-men, and so they couldn't be allowed to get hold of him. He knew that he couldn't afford to stay in the palace. Umbria had expected him, and that was bad; Celine had somehow escaped, and he needed to know where she was. He could do nothing for her if he was either locked up or embroiled in battle.

He also knew that, strong as the plant-men might be, he was both faster and smarter than they.

The plant-men approached from either side, stretching out their woody arms. Tomas waited until they had nearly reached him. He dropped to the ground, bruising his knees, and crawled through their legs faster than any man should be able to crawl. While they were still turning in confusion, he regained his feet and sprinted out the cell door.

He could hear Umbria roaring behind him as he leapt up the stairs. The plant-men were tripping over each other in their haste to track him down. He dashed through the palace halls and out through the yellow door into the courtyard. Plant-men were coming from every side, about fifteen of them. He ran for the door. It was shut and barred. The wooden bar across them looked as heavy as the gates themselves.

Tomas stopped and surveyed the wall. He squinted and cocked his head, studying its stones. The plant-men were slowing. They knew they had him cornered. He heard Umbria's heavy breathing and knew that he was advancing along with them.

Suddenly he saw—or felt—something in the wall that made him smile. He turned around, looked straight into Umbria's eyes, and said, "This wall was breached once."

Umbria was taken aback. "Yes," he began to say.

Tomas turned back around. From deep within him he summoned every ounce of magical strength he had. Then he rushed forward and hit the three-inch-thick stone wall with his shoulder.

In the charge he used all of his skill. Memory wakened in the wall that had once seen battle and fallen before it. The stone crumbled under his shoulder and then under the weight of his body as he pushed. He was through in a moment and running over the hill with all the speed of an Immortal, free and powerful like a streak of gold in the wind.

Tomas's feet carried him beyond the palace grounds, up the steep ridge where Umbria's sheep fed—he paused a moment to tell Aldon that he'd been to see Umbria and things had gone interestingly before blazing on—down the other side, around the base again (all this to make his trail much harder and slower to follow), through the woods, and down the town streets to Tereska's low door. This he banged on.

Tereska opened the door a crack and looked out at him over the chain locks. She slammed the door shut, clattered and clanked, and yanked Tomas inside. She stood with her back against the door and her astonishingly skinny arms crossed.

"What happened?" she asked.

"I need to find Celine," Tomas said. "The looking glass?"

To his surprise, Tereska didn't protest. She crossed the floor and took the blanket down, commanding Tomas over her shoulder to lock the door while he waited.

He did as she said. When he turned around, the looking glass was bare. His own face looked back at him from a pool of darkness. He leaned forward and stared intently into his own eyes. His surroundings melted away. He concentrated. Celine. He needed to see Celine. Not the courtyard or the guards, and not, please, crickets.

The scene that smoked into view was nothing he recognized. It was dark, but lit with an orange light. It seemed cavernous: a cave or perhaps a wide dungeon. It was hard to tell, because the view jerked from one side to another as though seen through the eyes of a small and nervous animal that was trying to watch every side of its surroundings at once.

When the view jerked left, it lit on something huge, dark, and faintly glowing. Tereska caught her breath and Tomas leaned forward for a better view, but the view flickered away again, to the far right this time, and he finally saw Celine. He didn't recognize her at first. She looked as though she'd been rolling in a pigsty. That wasn't, however, the most unusual thing about her. The most unusual thing was that she appeared to be dangling from the ceiling.

The eyes through which the mirror looked fixed themselves on Celine's precarious position. The view hyperfocused as though the eyes were dilating. And then, while Tomas and Tereska and the animal watched, Celine lost her grip and fell.

At that very instant a pounding on the door made both watchers jump and spin around, hearts beating so hard it hurt. Tomas realized his mistake too late and turned back, but the looking glass was dark. Frustrated, he blinked hard at his reflection several times, but the vision would not come back.

Tereska had grabbed a fire iron and held it ready to smash the head of anyone who came through the door. Judging from the pounding, the person outside wasn't anywhere close to getting in.

"Name yourself!" Tereska said.

"It's Aldon, fool woman!" came the shepherd's voice through the door. "Let us in!"

With an exasperated noise, Tereska threw the poker aside and started in on the locks again. The poker landed in a pile of dented pots with a crash. She threw the door open and let in Aldon and Brig.

"What be happening?" Aldon asked Tomas.

"We're going in, that's what's happening," Tereska said.

Immortal and shepherd boy looked askance at her. Even Brig looked dubious.

"What do ye mean?" Aldon asked.

"I mean, you'd best gather up the supplies," Tereska said. "The revolution is tonight."

"But—" Tomas said, trying to decide which of many "buts" to express. "There are only two of you."

"Three," Tereska corrected.

"Why now?" Aldon asked. "Three days ago ye wouldn't hear of goin' in there."

"I know," Tereska said. She looked back and forth between her companions and sighed. "You must think I've lost my nut. Well, listen. I saw that black thing in the looking glass. It was a dragon."

"We told ye it was a dragon," Aldon said.

" . . . and I said we hadn't the means to fight it," Tereska said. "Well, I was wrong. We have the means now and we may never have it again."

"What means?" Aldon asked. He sounded exasperated and ready to give up trying to follow Tereska's logic.

In answer, she pointed a long finger at Tomas. "Him."

Tomas started. "Me?" he asked.

"Don't tell me you can't fight a dragon," Tereska said. "You're an Immortal."

"Immortals can be killed," Tomas pointed out.

"But not easily," Tereska said. "Listen, you. Aldon and I have been planning this for years. We can deal with the pyrolines, with the plant-men, and with Umbria himself. If all goes well he'll not bother us—or the rest of this world—for a long time after tonight. But we can't deal with that dragon. That is your only task. Go face the dragon. Rescue Celine."

The blank mirror glimmered mockingly in the dark room. "I don't even know if Celine will live that long," Tomas said. They were the most miserable words that had ever passed his lips, but he recognized them as true.

"Then you can go avenge her," Tereska said. "Well?"

Tomas nodded. "I have to go in again anyway. We might as well go together."

Triumphantly, Tereska stuck her hand out. Tomas took it, and Aldon laid his rough hand over top. Brig barked.

"Tonight," Tereska said.

Chapter 11

UMBRIA WAS STARING AT HIS GATE-GLASS from his seat in a high-backed chair with velvet cushions. His feet were soaking in a pail of hot water. They were not especially sore or hard done by, but he liked to soak them when he was sulking.

Sulking he was now, in earnest. The memory breach had repaired itself after Tomas's exit. Umbria had magicked it to make sure it wouldn't fall again, and he had checked the rest of the wall besides. He hadn't known Tomas could work with memories. He cursed. That was a risky thing—very risky. Umbria's senses were limited when it came to memory, and who knew what unexpected opportunities it would open to that golden fool?

The gate-glass was a long, thin window in the middle of the room. It was propped up on a chair before the fire.

Through it Umbria could see the palace gates.

So he saw it when a broad-shouldered, bearded man approached the gate. His clothes were worn and threadbare. His shoes especially looked as though he'd journeyed long. In his hands he held something wrapped in cloth—something long and thin.

The man knocked at the gate. Umbria leaned forward. He cursed the dull plant-men for their inertia. Whenever they sat for any length of time they rooted themselves in the ground, which made them excruciatingly slow as doormen. The guard bird—result of Umbria's first successful attempt to turn a mammal into a non-mammal—started to bark and squawk in its nerve-jerking way.

The man kept knocking. The plant-men uprooted themselves after what seemed a small eon and moved to the door. They opened it and listened to the man's introduction. Umbria saw the man hold up the swathed thing. It looked like a sword.

It suddenly hit him that he couldn't count on the plant-men to let the man in, but he wanted to see him. He pulled his feet out of the hot water and bath salts, wrapped his robe tightly around himself, and swept down the hallway to the door, leaving damp footprints behind him.

Celine pushed herself halfway off the floor and stared. The dragon was sleeping. Through the tight cracks of its black scales, yellow light glowed. Smoke rose in thin spirals from its mouth and nostrils. It was huge. The cavernous room where she now crouched seemed made for it. It was vast—fifty feet in every direction, with a high roof. Embers in an enormous fireplace glowed on the other side of the dragon.

The cavern floor around the creature was littered with bones. Celine shuddered despite recognizing most of them—involuntarily—as having belonged to sheep and other such nonhuman creatures. The thought wasn't especially comforting. Just because the dragon hadn't made a habit of eating people didn't mean it might not start any day.

The question of how it had come to be here, and just how long it had been, jostled to the fore of Celine's mind. How in the name of all that was good had her uncle managed to acquire a dragon without her knowing it? Without her throwing a fit and utterly forbidding it?

Her eyes made the journey from the dragon's black, spiked tail, up its strangely glowing body, all the way to its head. She stared at the eyelid facing her—big as a grapefruit and blacker even than the rest of its body. The eye behind it also glowed, with a faint red light.

Then the eye opened and looked straight at her.

Celine froze. The eye was red, intelligent, and malevolent. The dragon hissed. Smoke slipped into the air from between its teeth.

Celine scanned the length of the hall. There—at the far end, a fifty-foot dash over the rocky floor, a door stood. Praying it would not be locked, she tensed her legs and prepared to bolt.

And then she remembered Winnie.

She looked up. Winifred had landed on a high stone pillar. Celine tried to catch her eye, but the wombat was absolutely rigid. Her pupils were dilated with fright. Her claws were clacking faintly against the stone. Celine swallowed a lump of frustration and fear. She knew that Winifred was outside herself with terror—that the nurse's sweet child could not overcome her animal instincts and save herself. It was too much to ask.

"Winnie!" Celine let the agonized sound out, hoping against hope for some response. There was nothing—from Winnie. But as soon as the word escaped her mouth, the dragon lifted its scaly, horselike head on its long, serpentine neck and swung it around so that both its red eyes were trained on Celine.

Celine stared back at it for a moment of dumb dread. Then she leaped aside—just in time. The dragon's head shot out, and its teeth snapped shut where she had just been. Celine scrambled to her feet and ran to the pillar. She jumped up, grabbing a handhold on the stone, and climbed as fast as she could manage. She saw the head coming for her again and swung herself around to the other side so that the dragon's nose collided with the pillar.

The pillar swayed from the impact. The cavern reeled all around her. Celine hauled herself up one more hand and snatched Winifred, stuffing her into her skirt pocket. The dragon head was coming for her again. She let go and fell to the stone floor, scrambling to her feet in the next moment and bolting toward the door.

A tremendous scraping and sense of motion filled the air. The dragon was moving, hauling itself out of its repose and getting ready to launch itself after its prey. Celine kept her eyes on the door and kept running. In her pocket, Winnie was still rigid. She was in an awkward position, and she slowed Celine down.

A whoosh of air. The smell of sulfur blew through the cavern as the dragon flapped its wings once. It landed in front of them, its claws sending bits of the stony floor flying. It turned on them and hissed, its mouth open and burning red, its teeth long and sharp. Celine skidded to a stop, the dragon's black scales and glowing underside burning themselves into her eyes. She turned and ran in the other direction: back toward the littered bones and the giant hearth.

The dragon came after them, but on its feet this time, more slowly. Its tail curled behind it. Its eyes were clever and pleased. It was playing with them.

In her pocket, Winnie started to tremble. Celine tripped over a ox's leg bone and skinned her mud-covered hands on the floor. She lurched forward again, casting a terrified look behind her. The wyrm was still advancing.

Celine looked around for any mode of escape. The door was out of the question. The dragon was blocking the way to it, and even if it wasn't, she had no prayer of getting that far without being overtaken. The hole in the ceiling through which she and Winnie had fallen was much too high for her to reach.

She turned away from the sight of approaching doom in

scales and a tooth-lined smile. Before her lay the giant hearth with its glowing embers, bones piled before it like an offering.

And, she realized with a spurt of hope that only the truly tenacious may feel, the way out.

Smoke from the dragon's mouth was curling around her ankles. She reached down and grabbed a long, thin bone, then ran forward, put the point of the bone on the rough ground, and vaulted into the fireplace.

Close up, there were three words to describe Malic: windblown, weather-beaten, and angry. Umbria chuckled at his own turn of phrase when he told himself that the man looked as though he'd been blown across the ocean by a magistral. The anger was unrelated to being windblown and weather-beaten and was solely due to the thick-headed way in which the plant-men would not let him in, answer his questions, or otherwise treat him as though he was anything other than a bush to be stared at.

Malic looked past the leafy heads of the plant-men when he heard a man's thin voice say, "They're easier to keep than people, but much more stupid." Before Malic had fixed his eyes on the strange little man who had appeared in the gate, the man was kicking and flailing at the plant-men. "Off with you! Out of my way, you ill-begotten vegetables."

The plant-men moved aside, and Malic found himself

face-to-face with the cunning little wizard-king whose name he knew to be Ignus Umbria, dressed in a bathrobe and sporting glistening feet with dust stuck to their damp soles.

"Who are you?" Umbria asked. "What do you want?"

"Are you Ignus Umbria?" Malic asked, even though he knew the answer.

"Don't waste my time," Umbria said. "You've seen my picture on the coins. You know who I am."

Malic grimaced. "Well, first off I want a bath," he said. "And a hot meal. And once you've coughed that up, I want an audience with you."

Umbria raised an eyebrow. "I'm not an innkeeper," he said. "Tell me why I shouldn't have my plant-men throw you in the dungeon." He paused when the word came out, and made a face as though the sound of "dungeon" was distasteful to him. "Or a tower."

Malic lifted up the cloth-swathed sword. "Because I'm an ally," he said. "If I wasn't, I wouldn't have brought you this."

"I don't need allies," Umbria said.

"But you've got one nonetheless," Malic said. His face was still a little red from anger with the plant-men, and now he seemed to be doing a concerted job of controlling himself.

"By virtue of what?" Umbria asked.

"Of common enemies," Malic said. His voice was growing more terse, like a balloon which can only handle a few milligrams more of air before it bursts, red and piecemeal, all over the place. "Tall skinny Immortal called Tomas."

Umbria smiled. The smile was entirely unexpected and therefore unnerving, but it also diffused some of Malic's buildup of air. At least he was getting somewhere.

"You have something against Tomas Solandis?" Umbria asked.

"He cheated me out of my life's work," Malic said. And then he called Tomas something not fit to be printed.

Umbria's smile grew. "You said enemies," he said. "There's another?"

"A cursed wench," Malic said. "Pretty girl, all too full of herself. When I finish snapping Solandis I'll grind her under my heel."

"You're too late," Umbria said. "She's been eaten by a dragon."

The news was shocking, so it took Malic a moment to regain himself. "That's . . . a pity," he said.

"More than you know," Umbria said, giving him a sharp look. "Celine was a thorn in a man's side, but not a bad child for all that. She got herself eaten; I wouldn't have done it to her."

Suddenly he stepped aside and motioned for Malic to come inside the courtyard. The plant-men closed the gates behind them, and the two men walked across the yard together. Malic walked with a latent weariness, still holding the sword carefully in his arms. Umbria tucked his hands into the bathrobe sleeves and spoke in the low tones of a conspirator.

"Mind you, Solandis doesn't know she's dead. He thinks she's escaped my dungeon, and he's sure to come looking for her in the palace somewhere. I don't know where or when, but when he comes I want to be ready for him." He cast a sidelong glance at Malic's bundle. "Will that help me?"

"Give me a bath and a meal," Malic said. "And I'll tell you."

"Very well," Umbria said. He chuckled. Out of the corner of his eye, Malic caught sight of something huge prowling in the corner of the courtyard: a black-and-orange pyroline the size of a lion. Despite himself, he shuddered.

Umbria ushered him through a yellow door. The weary traveler stepped into the luxury of the palace and inwardly sighed with relief.

Hot air rushed past her as Celine flew through the air, over the coals, straight for the uneven bricks at the back of the chimney. Several holes in the brick, handholds in case the need for chimney sweeping should arise, were just visible on the blackened surface. She grabbed them. The end of her dress trailed in the coals. The rising heat burned her legs, and she looked down to see a fire kindling at the end of the once-luxuriant cloth.

Still holding on with one hand, she used the other to pull up the length of cloth and fold it together, beating it against the wall in a desperate attempt to smother the flame. It worked. She heard a roar of air in the room as the dragon stopped crawling and flew toward the fireplace. Tucking the end of her skirt into her belt, she climbed the chimney as fast as she could. In a moment she was surrounded by stone. Smoke was drifting up the chute, but it was thin, and there was enough fresh air mixed with it that Celine didn't fear asphyxiation. She kept climbing.

Far, far above, she thought she could see light.

In her pocket, Winnie stirred. Her voice, high with fright and still trembling, said, "It's dark."

"We're in the chimney chute," Celine explained. "We're getting out."

"What if—" Winnie asked.

"Then we'll burn to cinders," Celine said. "Never mind that."

Of course she knew the dragon might just light a roaring fire in the fireplace beneath them—one high and hot enough to lick right up the chute and incinerate them both. But then again, it might not. It hadn't been quick to toast them in the hall. Maybe it didn't like its food flame broiled. Maybe they were just too much trouble.

It was, after all, a huge dragon. Enormous. A hundred times more destructive and terrifying than Umbria's pyro-lines.

"Where did he get it?" Celine burst out.

"What?" Winnie squeaked.

"That dragon," Celine said. She spoke through clenched teeth. Pulling herself and Winnie up the chimney was no easy task. "How in the name of all that's fair did he get a dragon?"

Winnie made no answer. Celine kept pulling: one hand after the other, one foot after the other. Higher and higher. If the dragon was moving below she had no idea; she could hear nothing in the chute but the curious whistling of air so common to long, vertical passages. At least it had not done anything yet.

After a few minutes she heard Winnie making a sound. It was not words or wombat squeaking. It sounded much like crying.

"What's wrong?" Celine asked.

"I'm sorry," Winnie said.

Celine paused and looked down at the grey lump in her pocket. Winnie had curled into a ball. Her nose was between her paws.

"It's not your fault," Celine said.

Winnie shook her head. "I'm no use for anything."

"Well, not for dragon slaying," Celine said. "Or running away. But it's not your fault. You're a faithful friend, Winnie. That's all I need right now."

Just when she thought her arms could not take it anymore, the patch of sky above them became brighter and bigger. They had emerged into a wider part of the chimney. This made ascent more difficult because Celine could no longer lean against the wall behind her, but the hand and footholds were bigger here, and freedom was so close that even Winnie poked her nose out of Celine's pocket and fixed her beady black eyes on the sky.

Malic was installed in a large porcelain tub full of steaming water and bubbles, where he happily lounged with the sword by his fingertips. Dinner was roasting, baking, and frying in the kitchen, and in the meantime Umbria had had a platter of bread, cheese, and wine set beside him.

Umbria himself sat outside the bath chamber door, drumming his fingers on a small gold table and talking through the door. He managed to get the whole story out of Malic, looking out the small window next to him to the courtyard whenever the mercenary started to ramble. High above, the guard bird let out a series of yaps that meant all was well beyond the gates.

"Where is the old man now?" Umbria interrupted when Malic told him of his arrival on the shore, when his boat had broken up on the shoals and he'd barely managed to swim to shore without being crushed to death.

"I don't know," Malic said. "Doesn't much matter. The old fool tottered off before I reached shore."

"It does matter," Umbria said. "It always pays to know what the enemy's doing."

"Monk ain't the enemy," Malic growled. "He's just a pawn. Used to be mine; now he's Solandis's."

Umbria knew better, but he decided not to share his wisdom with the bearded dolt behind the door. Pawns did not cross seas of their own volition to warn their masters of danger. Pawns did not overcome one-hundred-odd years of decrepitude to become heroes. Only people who loved did that. And if Umbria's years had taught him anything, it was that people who loved, while often predictable, were unmanageable and dangerous.

That had always been Celine's problem, he thought. The thought made him sorrowful. He didn't especially care for Celine, but all the same it was not nice that she should have been eaten. When the plant-men told him where the tunnel had led, and about the hole through which Celine had most certainly dropped, it had ruined his breakfast.

Malic was still talking. Rambling on now about the hazards at sea; about that cursed magistral which had, he was sure, tried to kill him. He was wrong again, Umbria reflected. If the magistral had tried to kill Malic, dead Malic would be.

He was distracted by a movement in the courtyard. A very strange movement. He frowned and looked harder. Something black, brown, and extraordinarily ragged was stomping across his courtyard, leaving filth in its wake on the smooth white cobblestones. In the corner of the yard, one of the pyrolines uncurled itself and yawned, stretching and then padding toward the strange figure. The figure stopped, turned, and hustled away in another direction. It disappeared from Umbria's view.

Before he could decide what to do about the apparition, the bath chamber door banged open. Malic stood before him, considerably fresher and more impressive than when he'd arrived, his thick brown hair and beard bushing in every direction. He wore a suit of golden clothes which Umbria had given him.

Umbria looked him up and down. "You're alive," he said. "I wouldn't have known it from the looks of you before." He held out a beautiful hand. "May I see it?" he asked.

Malic half-shoved the sword behind him. "Dinner first," he said.

Umbria's lip nearly curled. As if he would deny the man dinner—as if he were some common churl too stingy to feed an ally. If "ally" Malic could really be called.

"Dinner," he agreed with a slight smile.

Celine closed the green door behind her gently, trying to keep from slamming it. Her heart was pounding in her chest. Old fears died hard—the sight of the pyroline coming after her was at least as bad as the swoop of the dragon overhead. Winnie was not so paralyzed. She had poked her head all the way out of the pocket, and her claws rested on the edge of the cloth.

"Where are we going?" she wombat-whispered.

"My mother's rooms," Celine said. "I need new clothes."

She looked behind her. "Bother. These are leaving a trail." Mud and soot made a clear path all the way back to the door—and, she supposed, beyond it. She stopped a moment, thought, and then tossed Winnie out of her pocket and started to pull off her dress.

Winnie scrambled for a foothold on the smooth marble floor and looked up at Celine with wide eyes. "What are you doing?" she squeaked.

"Getting down to my underthings," Celine said. "We can't leave tracks behind us."

"Your feet will still leave marks," Winnie pointed out.

"I'll fix that," Celine said. She was down to her white under-dress now, which, while it was not caked with mud and soot, was still grimy. Her knee-length leggings were worse, and she started to pull them off too, and stuff them into a large flower vase on a table beside her.

"It isn't decent!" Winnie protested.

Celine shot her a scathing look as she shoved the last bit of lace inside the vase. "One can't always be decent!"

"But you're a princess," Winnie grumbled.

"And you're a seamstress," Celine answered back. "Who says fur is decent for a seamstress? You haven't worn clothes in years."

If wombats could blush, Winnie would have. She swallowed her objections and waddled after Celine as she ran on her toes down the hall. Dirty footprints still marked the floor behind her.

Celine picked up her pace, and Winnie scrambled to stay with her. "What about the footprints?" she gasped.

"The fountain ahead," Celine said.

Around a bend in the hall, a beautiful marble fountain waited. Celine duly hitched up the hem of her under-dress and danced through the water. Winnie climbed onto the edge of the fountain and nearly fell in after her, but she caught herself and glared at Celine, who was already climbing out the other side.

"You're still going to leave wet footprints," Winnie said.

"No, I'm not," Celine answered. She looked around, and her eyes lit on a small tapestry on the wall. She pulled it off, dried her feet and ankles, and carefully hung it back up. Then she bent down, scooped Winnie into her arms, and ran at top speed for the west side of the palace—and her mother's rooms.

Chapter 12

ON THE HILLSIDE OVERLOOKING THE PALACE, the revolution sat encamped among a herd of sheep. Brig lay at Aldon's feet, gently wagging the tip of his feathery tail while Tereska shoved the nose of a sheep who wanted to eat her plans aside for the sixth time.

"I still think I ought to have a dark cloak," Aldon complained.

Tereska sighed. "I told you this," she said. "I need one to get into Umbria's rooms. Tomas needs one because if Umbria sees him, the jig is up. You don't need one because you're no one special, and because you need to be seen."

Aldon shut his mouth and looked annoyed, but not to any unwarranted measure. He had two large sacks tied around his waist. One moved if he sat still too long, with a multilegged crawling movement that gave him the jitters. The other was heavier and gave off a slight powder if he jolted it. It also stank. His job, easily the most dangerous of the bunch, was also the least glamorous—hence his disappointment at being denied a dark cloak.

"A dark cloak," he reflected, "would make a man feel more a hero and less a gardener, if ye know what I mean."

Tomas winked. "But it's the truer hero who will go in without protection," he said.

"I suppose."

"Now, listen you," Tereska said, jabbing a stick at Tomas. "You know your job. No revealing yourself. No looking for Celine. Nothing at all but hiding until the dragon makes an appearance."

"You've told me three times," Tomas said.

"No, but I don't trust you," she answered. "You're a man in love and Immortal besides."

"What does that have to do with it?" Tomas asked.

"I never trust Immortals," Tereska said. "Haven't had enough experience with them to know they're trustworthy."

"You don't have enough experience to know we're not," Tomas argued.

Tereska gave him a look which informed him his argument was, in her consideration, very poor. And after all, it was.

He bit back any protest. She was right. If he appeared, all attention would be diverted to him and Tereska wouldn't get what she needed: Umbria's ire and attention, entirely focused on her. And if he went looking for Celine, he might not be of any use when the dragon put in an appearance.

He was partially hopeful that the dragon wouldn't appear, but it didn't seem likely. A man like Umbria didn't acquire a secret weapon like that and not use it when his sanctum was invaded.

Finished giving her instructions, Tereska took a deep breath and then held out her hand, palm up. Aldon laid his hand in hers, and Tomas laid his over both of theirs. His hand was wide and sun-brown, and he closed his fingers over the hands beneath his and smiled. They were brave hands. Foolish hands, perhaps, but skillful and courageous, and Tomas felt privileged to be with them.

Then they three let go and stood, looking down the ridge to the palace. The sheep around them baaed and tinkled the bells on their collars. Aldon called Brig to heel. The collie jumped up and stood at his master's side.

The time had come.

Finished his meal at last—beef and eggs, fried sausages and patties of fried bread, cups of cold water and hot mead and coffee, vats of honey and pureed squash—Malic looked up with an expression of unmatched satisfaction and said, "You rulers eat well."

"We do," Umbria said. Then he folded his arms and said, "And now the game is up, my friend. Show me what you've brought me so that I may decide whether you'll stay another night here or in the . . . tower."

Malic looked up with some alarm. "I'm your ally," he said.

"I have yet to decide that," Umbria said. He wasn't smiling. He enjoyed the effect that his unwonted sternness had on the scheming oaf.

Without another word, Malic wiped his mouth on his sleeve and reached down to retrieve his bundle from beside his feet. While Umbria watched, he untied the bits of leather that bound the cloth and then unfolded it. A white scabbard and golden hilt became visible. Umbria's eyes glinted. Malic laid the sword in his palms and held it out.

Umbria picked up the sword with a look of barely concealed awe. The sword was a thing of immense beauty and craftsmanship. He drew it, drinking in the way the light danced on the fine silver blade. And then he saw the smudged writing on the hilt.

"Umbria's Bane," he read aloud. His voice was taut with wonder. "A marvel," he said. "A work of art."

"It was Solandis's," Malic pointed out. "His Immortal gift, if I'm not mistaken. To kill you with."

"Of course that's what it is," Umbria said. His voice was impatient. He disliked Malic showing off his knowledge, pretending to tell him what he already knew. "But look at it, man! It's glorious."

"And it's yours," Malic pointed out uneasily.

"Yes," Umbria said. "Thank you, my friend." He turned the sword again so he could watch the sun dance off it and cast light on the ceiling and walls.

"One thing I don't understand," Malic charged on. "If he knew he was coming to face you, why didn't he bring the sword?"

"Because he's a coward," Umbria said. "He's been avoiding me all his life. He doesn't want to force a confrontation. He hoped to come and rescue Celine and get her out without having to kill me."

"Stupid fellow," Malic snorted. "He could be a hero."

Umbria shot fire at Malic. "You don't know what you're talking about," he said. "If Tomas kills me he'll lose everything."

Confusion was apparent in the bearded man's face. Umbria explained. "When one Immortal kills another, he loses his immortality," he said. "I don't want to kill him either."

"Then why not give him the girl and send him away?" Malic blurted. Too late he remembered that Celine was dead—but his question still held. Why hadn't Umbria done that in the first place?

"Because I don't like knowing he's alive," Umbria said. "He haunts me. I dream his face at night. I am a man of science and an explorer of magic. I find delight in a million different things. I want the freedom to explore them without the face of Solandis over my shoulder—the threat of defeat always at my heels. He doesn't want to face me, but he will someday. I want him to do it now. On my terms."

"And you'll kill him?" Malic asked.

"No, fool," Umbria said. "What good is freedom if I lose my immortality? I'll deal with him. I'll see to it that he can't threaten me."

"That sword," Malic said, smacking his mouth at some taste that still lingered. "That sword will help you."

"Perhaps," Umbria said. His tone suddenly changed. He sounded as if he was addressing a very small and ignorant boy. "You have done well," he said.

The guard bird looked down from its lofty post and saw a thick-shouldered boy creeping along the wall of the palace with a black-and-white collie close at his heels. To the bird's sharp eyes it seemed that the shadows around the boy were behaving peculiarly, but though it swooped down for a closer look, it could not make them take shape as anything more than bumptious shadows.

This confused the guard bird, which felt that it ought to bark an alarm but didn't know what to bark an alarm at. The boy at least had substance, as did his dog. The guard bird opened its beak to start barking, but in that moment the boy looked straight at it and said, "Heel!"

This knocked the guard bird right off kilter. When it

had been a dog in the court of Umbria it had been an exceptionally well-trained one, and when someone said "Heel!" in that tone of voice, the thing to do was heel. Of course, one didn't usually obey strangers, but no one had acted as master to the guard bird in a very long time. Umbria and the plantmen, even Celine, had largely ignored it, letting it eat crickets and fly around the palace walls, and cursing at it whenever it barked. Winifred had always been kind to the dog when it was still a dog, but she was turned into a wombat shortly before the guard dog was turned into a guard bird, and wombats were not especially friendly either to dogs or birds. The bird's still-strong doggy instincts craved a master, wanted a master, longed for a master.

It heeled. It swooped down and made a very clumsy landing next to the collie, flapping its big white wings and trying to get a firm footing on the ground. The boy reached into his pocket, pulled out a dog biscuit, and fed it to the bird, which snatched it up with evident joy. The boy scratched its head and said, with a grin, "Good dog."

Aldon stood out of his crouch and shook his head as he watched the big white bird try to get the dog biscuit down its gullet. If he hadn't sometimes heard the bird barking over the hillside where he grazed the sheep, he would never have believed Tereska's story of its origin. He turned and resumed his creeping along the wall. Brig followed, so close that his wet nose sometimes touched Aldon's heel. The bird left what remained of the biscuit and waddled along behind.

A few feet back, two human-shaped shadows came apart from the wall and crept along behind them. Had the guard bird looked around, it would have clearly seen two pairs of high boots and two black face masks with slits for eyes, seemingly walking along disembodied. Every other part of Tomas and Tereska was wrapped in the dark cloaks.

They were on the back side of the castle, far away from the front gates and the guard rooms where the plant-men mostly loitered. On the other side of the wall was a sheepfold, where Aldon took his charges late every day and found them again early every morning. He found the low wooden door in the wall and unlocked it. Brig and the bird stayed at his heels, so he let Tereska and Tomas go before him, then came through and shut the door.

The sheepfold was surrounded by high stone walls painted with lime. The floor was dirt and littered with the evidence of sheep: dung, clumps of wool, and hoofprints. Aldon led them across the small expanse to a very large stone in the wall. At first glance there was nothing unusual about this stone. It sat snugly in the wall just like all the other stones, though it did seem to stand out in slightly sharper relief. Closer inspection revealed that the mortar around it had been almost all chipped away.

Aldon gestured to the stone with as much flourish as he could manage. He was proud of it. He'd been working at the mortar all year, the chipping muffled by the sound of baaing sheep, and no one else had seen his handiwork until now.

With a look at each other, the two shadows rushed forward and put their shoulders to the stone. It moved without too much trouble: straight through the wall and out the other side. The opening it left was big enough for one person to fit through at a time, and it led into a roofed passageway on the north side of the courtyard.

The shadows slipped through, one after the other. Aldon made his awkward passage next. Brig bounded in behind him, and then the guard bird hopped into the gap, waddled through, and hopped out again. It let out a tiny bark of joy. Aldon shot a disapproving look at it. It snapped its beak shut.

The stone roof of the passageway cast deep shadows, rendering Tereska and Tomas almost invisible. Even though Aldon knew they were there, the sound of Tereska's voice startled him.

"Good luck," she said. And then she swept off. Tomas likewise turned away, and Aldon could just see his boots walking lightly down the stones.

Turning back to his own task, he surveyed the courtyard. The gardens stirred in a slight breeze. A burst of water shot up from the fountain with an explosive gurgle. At first he mistook the plant-men on the far side of the courtyard, near the gate, for more gardens. But then one of them stood up and walked a few paces, and he knew better. The plant-men, for all that they were nothing but glorified rosebushes, were unnerving to look at. Aldon swallowed, wishing his mouth wasn't so dry, and kept sweeping the courtyard with his eyes.

There. The pyrolines were both there, sleeping in the sun with their heads on each other's backs. Now Aldon's mouth was *really* dry. Tereska's warnings hadn't really prepared him for how big they were—or how powerful-looking. Beside him, Brig growled. He had seen them too. Aldon reached into the heavy pouch at his waist and fingered the dry powder inside. This, he thought, had better work.

Being sure to stay hidden in the shadows, he drew out a handful of the power and rubbed it on his neck and behind his ears. It was light brown and made him look like a little boy who'd been playing in the dirt. He whistled lightly, calling Brig to him. The guard bird hopped up after him. He rubbed powder behind Brig's ears and dusted his coat and tail with it, then did the same for the bird—admiring the way the powder clung to its slightly oily feathers. Brig snuffed and shook his head, showing his annoyance.

"Just a precaution, boy," Aldon whispered.

He squinted into the sunshine, trying to get a view of the pyrolines' faces. He thought their eyes were closed; their breathing heavy with sleep. The spurting fountain, acting particularly stagnant, was a good thirty paces away. Beyond it, the plant-men were still loitering. For a few more minutes at least, everything in the courtyard was still and sluggish in the hot sun.

He wondered where Tereska was.

He hated waiting.

The dark cloak wanted to melt into anything of a dark hue: carpets with patches of purple, deep red, or black; tapestries with funereal weavings or night scenes; dark wooden flourishes along the wall and ceiling; suits of black armour; and of course, the shadows. It was distracting to run along the halls and watch oneself become attuned to a thousand little darknesses—so distracting that Tereska forgot to watch where she was going and nearly slipped on a muddy patch on the floor. She didn't take the time to wonder why there was mud on the floor, but fixed her eyes on the goal and kept going, ignoring the dark cloak with all of its shifting.

She knew where she was going. As a washerwoman she had known these halls more intimately than anyone: every crack and crevice of them belonged to her. She knew the undersides of the carpets and the walls back of the tapestries. And because she was not just a washerwoman but also a born thief, spurred on by a noble cause—because she was attentive and in fact snooping by nature—she knew where the entrance to Umbria's secret vault, where he kept his most valued treasures, lay. She had been in there once before, just long enough to snatch the dark cloaks and use them to carry the looking glass away—though the looking glass had not been in the vault, but in Umbria's bath chamber, and she had snatched it out from the steamy air while another servant was running the water and Ignus Umbria himself was banging about in the changing-closet only inches away.

Voices in the hall startled her. Someone was coming—more than one. Not plant-men, because they were talking. As the voices drew nearer, she recognized the tones of Ignus Umbria. His companion grunted in reply. They were coming straight toward her.

Tereska looked around frantically. A few steps in the direction she had come, three suits of armour stood posed for attack. Tereska stood close to the biggest one, an eight-foot figure in black armour. Its arms came around either side of her, and she stood stiff as a lance. The voices were getting louder.

A moment later Umbria swept into view, with a tall, big-shouldered, bearded man by his side. The man looked like an oaf, and Tereska's lip would have curled if she wasn't so afraid that Umbria would look down and notice the extra pair of boots standing amidst the armour.

He didn't. They carried on past her. She breathed a sigh of relief—and then stiffened again, her spine straight as a fireplace poker.

She had heard, clearly and distinctly, the sound of a breath behind her.

Was it her imagination, or had the suit of armour's arms moved in closer?

Tereska turned around very slowly and looked into the giant headpiece. Through the barred visor, a pair of crystal blue eyes looked out at her.

They blinked.

Tereska took one hasty step backwards, outside of the arms' reach, turned around, and fled.

Celine stood in her under-dress with one bare foot on the edge of her mother's cedar chest, hauling out dresses, holding them up to the light, and discarding them behind her with the swift efficiency of a woman with no patience for frills. Her mother had loved to look beautiful, and while Celine certainly did not object to it, the lace and bows and puffs and sashes favoured by the previous generation would not aid her in her present aim—which was, of course, to do something about her uncle so he couldn't keep carrying on and hurt Tomas.

Winnie, who had been dodging flying articles of clothing but had not escaped the latest shawl in time, let out a sad sigh from beneath its fringes.

"It all brings back such memories," she said, looking around the empty chambers. Except for the thin layer of dust on everything, especially visible now that Celine had dashed the curtains open, the old days might still live in those rooms. Winifred might still be a sweet little golden child, traipsing around after her nursemaid mother and getting constantly underfoot. Celine's mother might still be sitting in the velvet chair by the window, sighing slightly and smiling down at Winnie as she scrambled on her hands and knees to pick up the spools of thread she'd managed to spill. Celine's mother, Winnie thought, had always been most condescending in her smiles, and in the advice she had often given concerning Winnie's upbringing.

"You mustn't worry too much about the child," Celine's mother would say to the nurse, even as she sighed. "Time must improve her."

Whether wombats were generally quick criers or not Winifred didn't know, but thoughts of the old days often brought tears to her eyes, and now was no exception. She marveled that Celine could go through the old chest of clothes with such cavalier indifference.

Celine looked up just at that moment and saw the tear in the corner of Winnie's marblelike eye. She understood it, because she lowered the pink flounced dress she was at that moment inspecting and cocked her head imploringly. "It's not that I'm coldhearted, Winnie, really I'm not. There's just too much else to think about right now. If I let myself start mourning I'll never help Tomas."

Winnie nodded and looked off in the distance, then absently scratched her ear. A moment later Celine's words sunk in. "Help Tomas?" she asked. "How are we going to do that?"

"By sending my uncle away," Celine said. "He's gotten right out of hand. It's got to stop before someone gets hurt."

Winnie looked down at her furry, clawed paws, and said, "But how are we going to . . ."

"The Machine," Celine said. One look from her silenced any protests Winnie might have considered squeaking out. "And then," Celine said, her eyes still warning Winnie to behave, "we're going to send that dragon to the moon. I'll never be able to handle the beast if it gets hungry."

All at once Celine snatched a dress from the bottom of the chest, said, "This'll do," and disappeared behind the oriental screen that stood in the corner. She reappeared minutes later, tying a sash around her waist. The dress was long and simple, yet on Celine it was stunning. The material was a rich ivory trimmed with blue.

Winnie looked up at her with sparkling eyes and said, "You look like a queen."

Celine smiled down at her friend. For a bare minute they stood thus regarding each other, and then Celine swept Winnie up onto her shoulder and whirled out of the room with the grace of a warrior maiden going forth to face her foes.

Chapter 13

WHEN THE SUN ROSE THAT DAY, it was over a world in which many out-of-the-ordinary things would take place. It rose over a world where children were born and elderly people died; where, more strangely, some children died and some elderly people were born anew. It rose over a world where flowers would grow out of ashes and crickets learn to sing. It rose over a world where a gull might forget how to fly or a wind might chuckle to itself—even a great, fierce star wind—over some secret doing.

Of all the things happening in the world beneath the sun, the things happening in the palace of Ignus Umbria, Immortal, were not least among the strangest.

Ignus Umbria himself did not know anything out of the usual was happening—out of his usual, anyway—until a tall, skinny woman with red hair stood on the ramparts of the wall, threw off her dark cloak, and let out a war whoop that echoed all through the halls and over the courtyard of the palace.

Umbria happened to be standing before a window across the courtyard at the time. He looked out to see Tereska, her long red hair blowing wildly in a sudden wind, holding something up that caught the sunlight and reflected it back at him. He squinted until he recognized it, then turned red and hung himself half out the window, pointing up at Tereska.

"Guards!" he shouted. "Get that woman!"

At this Tereska grinned a terrifying sort of smile, turned, and disappeared. She had in fact thrown the cloak back over herself while dropping to her knees on the ramparts so that she seemed to melt right into the stones. The object she had held up was now inside the cloak, where she held it tightly with one hand and crawled on the other.

The object now nestled close to Tereska's beating heart was a lantern. It looked much like any lantern, with a frame of beaten brass and six sooty glass panes. Inside, a fire was burning. To the ignorant it did not look like a prize worth stealing, but Tereska was not ignorant. She knew full well that what she held in her hands was Ignus Umbria's original tongue of Ravening Fire, without which he could create no more.

And she knew how much he liked to play with fire.

Down in the courtyard, the plant-men had stirred themselves at Umbria's shouts, and as he continued to rain down abuse on them before pulling his head back through the window and disappearing from sight, they uprooted themselves with all the speed they could muster. They made a groaning sound as they did so, the sort of sound that very old and large trees make when the wind bends them. Normally they did not root so deeply, but it was a beautiful hot sort of day, and they had all been photosynthesizing for all they were worth.

They turned almost as one and were greeted by the excited barking of a black-and-white sheepdog which stood directly in their path, wagging its feathery tail and grinning at them. A stocky boy stood next to it, with a white bird on his shoulder and both his hands inside a sack tied to his waist.

The plant-men began to move forward with malice in their steps. Aldon let them come a few steps closer and then pulled his hands out of the bag, spraying its contents up in the air. A cloud of tiny, reddish spots rose in fistfuls and fell upon the advancing enemy. The plant-men took one more step forward and staggered to a halt almost as one. The central among them, showered most liberally by the cloud, fell to the ground and began to thrash its arms and legs in silent agony. Aldon threw several more handfuls, aiming them at the plant-men still standing, and at last shook out his bag, letting the wind blow its last remaining contents at the guards.

Aphids, Aldon thought, were remarkable.

Behind him, the guard bird kicked up a terrible squawking. Brig's deep, growling barks joined it a second later. Aldon whirled around, dropping the empty aphid bag.

The pyrolines had awakened and were stalking toward him, eyes glowering.

Aldon looked up to the palace wall, silently praying for Tereska, and then grabbed the second pouch from his waist and tore a path to the fountain. One of the pyrolines broke into an easy run, halting in his path. Aldon skidded to a stop and looked frantically around him. The other pyroline was still coming leisurely toward him.

Suddenly, Brig dashed through Aldon's legs and ran straight for the pyroline, barking, growling, and showing his teeth. The pyroline drew back a moment, jumping away from the black-and-white bullet. Then it snarled and pounced.

Half in despair, Aldon watched as Brig and the pyroline closed in combat. The next second, something seemed to catch the pyroline off guard. It yowled and pulled away, pawing at its nose in a most peculiar fashion. Trusting that his plan was working, Aldon gripped the pouch even more firmly, took a deep breath, and ran to the fountain. He jumped up on its marble side and sloshed through the water, climbing the statuary to the very top. Then he turned the pouch over and dumped its entire contents down the fountain's spout. Overhead, the guard bird was having fits. He turned and dashed back through the water toward his dog, who was now circling the confused pyroline and had a slash in his black shoulder to show for his courage. Brig did not see—or could not react—to the other pyroline, which was approaching behind him with its tail slowly curling in the manner of all cats before they pounce on their prey.

"Brig!" Aldon shouted. His voice cracked with the force of his cry. In that moment, the fountain behind him exploded. Its burst of water was louder, higher, and more exuberant

than usual. And it sprayed the powder into the air, ont(
courtyard walls, and all over the white flagstones.

Both pyrolines halted in their tracks as the wet powder
came down on them. One of them began to mewl horribly,
and the bigger one rolled its eyes. They opened their mouths
and panted. They ran in circles and hopped in the air. They
began to frisk and to scamper in a way that is cute when
kittens do it, but somehow terrifying when the playful are
pyrolines.

Aldon whistled. Brig pulled himself away from the giant
cats and came panting to his master's feet. Aldon patted his
head, his eyes still trained on the frolicking giants.

Tereska had paid as much as two months' rent for the
catnip powder. Aldon had called her several names when he
found about it, but she swore it would work.

She was right.

Tomas was searching for the dragon when he came upon
Malic in a corridor near the dungeon. This startled him almost as badly as it did the bearded man—though it took
Malic longer to recognize him. Tomas had taken off his face
mask so as to see better in the shadows, but much of him was
still hidden by the dark cloak.

"What are you looking for?" Malic demanded. His face
was red, partially because he'd been caught off his guard, and

partially because he'd just been into Umbria's wine stores.

Tomas didn't answer.

Malic laughed loudly. "Looking for that girl, are you? You're too late. She's dead. The dragon got her."

In that moment, something unexpected happened.

Tomas's heart broke.

Of all the things the sun saw that day, an Immortal's heartbreak was the saddest of them. Tomas stood as still as a statue. He did not respond outwardly to Malic's words. To him all the spinning of the universe suddenly became noticeable, and he felt dizzy. The bully stared at him a few moments, and then began to laugh again.

"Can't even swear vengeance?" Malic said. "Swear, turn colour, something? Some Immortal you are." He spat. "You're hardly even a man."

Tomas licked his lips. They were terribly, terribly dry. They tasted like ash. He was beginning to grow hot, though he didn't know it, and to radiate awful energy, as though he was himself a sun—as though the worlds that orbited around him were about to be thrown off course. The dark cloak slipped from his shoulders and fell on the floor. Something kindled in his immortal eyes, and Malic saw it. He turned grey behind his thick beard. Suddenly he realized his mistake.

"Where is Umbria?" Tomas asked.

Malic pointed a shaky finger. "Up there somewhere. Something's going on . . . he marched off in a rage."

Tomas bowed his head slightly. He turned to go. He paused and looked back with a strange, curious detachment at Malic once more, as if he would ask him something. But he did not. Instead, he turned and walked out of the room, and the walls around him shifted as though turned into a mirage by the shimmering heat waves of the sun.

"Where are my lackeys?" Umbria bellowed as he ran up the hallway. He stopped at a cross-corridor, looking both ways with his brows knit together. "What good are lackeys if they don't come when you call?"

He rushed to the window and looked out. His eyes fell upon his squadron of plant-men in what appeared to be death agonies and his giant pyrolines apparently ready to pass out from pleasure. A stocky boy followed by a dog and a bird was sneaking out of their midst.

An ear-piercing whoop from the end of the hallway all but made Umbria jump out of his skin. He whirled around. The skinny woman was standing there again, holding up the lantern full of Ravening Fire.

"You!" Umbria burst out. "I know you! Thieving washer-woman." He took a menacing step forward, holding out his smooth craftsman's hand.

"Give it here," he said, his voice almost sniveling. "Give it here and I'll let you go."

Tereska nearly answered back, but then saw the way Umbria's fingers were curling and realized he was muttering to himself. Heart suddenly in her throat, she threw the dark cloak around her again. In the next instant it turned to dust and floated away around her.

Umbria cackled. "You thought I was about to turn you into something, didn't you? Well, you're next. Hand it over!"

Tereska wordlessly shook her head, then dashed down the cross-corridor. Umbria did not even curse her footsteps. Instead, he followed at a leisurely pace. She was headed for the north tower. Even a fool could see why, he thought—and he was not a fool.

Nor was he half so desperate to retrieve the Ravening Fire as Tereska thought he was. If he had been, her plan might have worked. As it was—as it was, Umbria reflected, it could only serve to prove the point that one must never underestimate one's enemies. The Machine was in the north tower, and Tereska evidently hoped to lure him into it. Heaven only knew where she planned to send him. It didn't matter.

He wasn't going.

Tereska was halfway down the hallway, aware through the intensity of her concentration that Umbria was not far behind her, when Tomas stepped out of a door between her and Umbria. He was not the same Tomas who had come into her house with Aldon only a few days ago. Tereska stopped and turned around to stare at him. She could not tear her eyes away. Neither, she somehow managed to notice, could Umbria.

And no wonder. Tomas was terrifying.

Time itself seemed to halt as he stepped into the hall. Everything around him blurred. He seemed to be the only real thing in the room, a creature full of immense and terrible energy—and all of it was directed at Umbria. Tereska pulled the ragged cloak she'd worn beneath the dark cloak around her, drawing her stolen treasures close. She felt like a shadow in a world that was about to explode, but the things she held beneath her cloak gave even shadows some tiny measure of power.

"Umbria!" Tomas said. His voice didn't sound like him. The floor and the walls vibrated as he spoke. "Umbria, it is the Day of Reckoning."

"No," Umbria stammered. "No, boy, stand back. You don't want to destroy me."

Tomas's eyes looked as though fires were burning in them. These were not the old welcoming candles that had so comforted Celine, nor the dancing flickers that had enchanted many a man or woman before. This was a destructive fire, a hot, searing one; a fire that came out of Tomas's heart—and his heart was doing what it had never done before.

Tomas stared at Umbria. His voice shook. "You're wrong," Tomas said. "I never wanted to destroy you before. But I do now."

Umbria's fingers were all twitching, all ten of them doing a staccato dance. Incantations tumbled through his brain: formulas and scientific mumblings that he'd carefully learned for just such a time as this. He spoke one under his tongue, barely forming the words but throwing his will into them, and then he pointed up and shouted a word.

Lightning jumped from his fingertips and shot across the room. It hit a vase behind Tomas. The glass shattered.

"Blast!" Umbria exclaimed. "How could I have missed?"

He looked up at Tomas again. He had taken a step closer, and the boiling energy in the air around him made Umbria tremble. "Get back, boy!" he shouted. "Get back. You can't destroy me. You're unarmed. You're unprepared. I'll feed you to the dragon, so help me!"

Tomas's eyes narrowed. "As you did Celine?" he said. His voice was choked.

Understanding flared inside Umbria. "That was an accident!" he exclaimed. "She tunneled her own way into the dragon's cave, curse her." He was backing away now, looking around him for an escape route, drawing nearer to a black suit of armour with a battle-axe in its hand. "Don't ask me why she took it into her head to dig—she's always been stubborn and headstrong and I—"

He paused, and for a moment something human came into his face and halted Tomas. "I'm sorry it happened," Umbria said. "I wouldn't have done it to her."

Tomas looked aside for a brief moment, and then he said, "But she's dead. And it is—it is—your fault."

Umbria saw his chance. He spun around and grabbed the shaft of the battle-axe, intending to wrench it away from the suit of armour, magic it, and hurl it across the room at his adversary. If he could just animate the thing, it would keep Tomas busy enough to let Umbria get away without killing the young Immortal—to let him get away long enough to come up with some kind of plan.

Two things happened to prevent this. First, the suit of armour tightened its hold on the battle-axe and refused to let go. While Umbria dealt with the shock of this unexpected turn, a voice interrupted the scene. An old, quaking, humble voice. It said, "Sun-God?" And it sounded very dismayed.

The voice, as quiet and weak as it was, arrested Tomas more than any war cry could have done. He halted and spun around. Coming into the corridor behind him was Grandfather Monk: as old, bent, and watery-eyed as ever, but with something noble and sweet in his face that was even greater than what had been there before. His hair was all standing on end as though it had been shaped that way by a very powerful wind. The little pyroline came from between his ankles and mewed. It looked up at Tomas with a reproving expression in its smoky eyes.

Umbria saw all this and tried one more time to pull the battle-axe free, but this time the suit of armour not only tightened its hold, it pulled back. It was so strong that it wrenched the axe entirely free from Umbria's grasp. Umbria nearly went sprawling, but he caught his balance, looked wildly between the suit of armour and the still-distracted Tomas, and sprinted away down the hall and through the nearest door.

"Tomas?" Monk said. He reached out toward Tomas. His fingers were shaking. He looked afraid and awestruck all at once.

"Why did you call me Sun-God?" asked Tomas.

"I . . . you . . . well," Monk said. "You look like one."

Tomas stepped forward as though to lay his hand on Monk's shoulder, but Monk shrunk away from him, and the pyroline hissed and let out its claws as if to defend the old man.

Tomas cocked his head. "Are you afraid of me?" he asked.

Monk's watery eyes watered harder than ever. "Yes?" he said.

In that moment all the fearsome, raging, sunlike energy went out of Tomas. The shimmering edges of the room ceased to shimmer. His voice no longer made the floors quake. He was suddenly and entirely himself. The fires that were burning in his eyes turned into embers. Sad embers.

"I'm sorry," he said. "Don't be afraid of me."

His voice sounded so wounded, so pleading, that Monk shook his head in mute protest and wrapped his arms around the tall Immortal. The pyroline meowed happily.

Tereska cleared her throat. She was not looking at either of the men. She raised a long, thin finger and pointed.

"Tomas," she said with remarkable control, "that suit of armour is about to kill you."

Tomas grabbed Monk under the arms and leaped aside like a giant grasshopper. The battle-axe crashed down and embedded itself in the floor just where they had been standing.

The suit of armour tore its helmet off, freeing a ruggedly handsome head with a black, curly beard and piercing blue eyes. "Untruth!" protested the suit—now revealed to be, for whatever immensely odd reason, a man. His voice boomed. "I intended to tap him on the shoulder. Speak not so rashly, fair lady!"

Tereska raised an eyebrow. "Fair lady, my foot," she said. "I'm a thief and a washerwoman, and don't you forget it."

The suit of armour bowed. "And a great magician," he said.

"I am not!" Tereska protested.

Tomas took this opportunity to interrupt the conversation. "Who are you?" he asked.

"My name is Sir Brian de la Roche," the newcomer said. His blue eyes narrowed. "Who are you?"

"Not important," Tomas said, ignoring the fact that every extenuating circumstance suggested otherwise. "Are you on Umbria's side?"

The blue eyes became instantly scornful. "No."

"Good," Tomas said. He stuck out his hand. "Allies, then."

Sir Brian shook Tomas's hand with an uncertain air. He looked over at Tereska, who was growing more impatient by the second.

"Is this man your ally?" he asked.

"Yes," she snapped. "And he's Immortal. And we are running out of time."

On his mad dash through the halls of his palace, a disconcerted Ignus Umbria passed a window where he witnessed his plant-men still fighting off some invisible attack and his pyrolines apparently suffering the aftereffects of hyperventilation—they were heaped on top of each other in the middle of the courtyard, panting.

This reminder of the revolution gave more purpose to his mad dashing. That wild skinny thief, and presumably the shepherd her apprentice, wanted him to go to the north tower where the Machine was. Duly, that was where he would go.

Cackling to himself, he half-ran, half-skipped up the tower. He had been caught by surprise, but this was still his palace. His territory. And the north tower was more than usually his territory.

He burst through the door of the tower and tripped headlong over a grey, furry animal on the floor. He jumped up with a curse, pulled his hand back with the intent of turning the animal into a footstool, and set his eyes fully on Celine.

"You!" he burst out, forgetting the animal altogether. Celine was standing outside the rim of the Machine, evidently trying to make sense of its controls. She looked as surprised to see him as he was to see her.

Except, of course, that he had thought she was dead. It

is always more surprising to see a dead person alive than it is to see a live person not dead.

Ignus Umbria did two contradictory things in the second that followed. He said, "Thank God you're alive." And then he twittered all of his fingers, pointed, shouted a word, and sent a bolt of lightning at Celine. She ducked. It hit a piece of the wall and shattered it.

"Curses!" Umbria shouted. "How did I miss?"

He leaped forward, and Celine dodged him by jumping into the Machine. He circled her, and she circled him, while energy crackled in the Machine and both of them looked nervous.

"Don't you touch me, Uncle," she said. "This has all got to stop."

"It's too late, my girl," Umbria said. "Things are out of hand. Do you know what sort of riffraff are overrunning my palace?"

"Riffraff!" Celine exploded. "You have a dragon in the dungeon! Do you know you have a dragon in the dungeon? Of course you do! What are you thinking?"

Umbria might have answered, but they would never know, because in that moment he tripped over Winnie again and hit the floor of the Machine with his unhappy face.

Celine leapt for the Machine controls and pulled the first lever she touched. Six strands of blue light shot down from the top of the Machine, coiled together, crackled, and hit Ignus Umbria right between the shoulder blades.

He disappeared.

Celine held her breath for a full minute before she realized she was doing it. Then she let it out, looked down at Winnie, and said, "We did it?"

Winnie scratched her ear in reply. They stared at each other. Things had happened too quickly.

Then a sound like light fizzing sounded sharply, and the blue bolts jumped out and tangled themselves again. The room was suddenly plunged into darkness. Celine was thrown backward by a rush of air. She collided with a piece of furniture that wrenched her shoulder. Holding it, she stood up slowly.

"Winnie?" she said.

There was no answer. Celine had a terrible sense that something was in the room. Her voice trembled this time. "Uncle?"

In answer, something took a deep, slow breath. As the breath let out, a burning light flared up.

Pale golden light, slipping out from underneath the tight cracks of hard black scales.

In the darkness, her uncle cackled.

Chapter 14

OUT IN THE COURTYARD, ALDON HAD HIDDEN HIMSELF behind a low stone wall where he could watch the results of his efforts. The pyrolines made him nervous—the aphids might eat the plant-men completely, for all he knew, but the catnip was bound to wear off eventually. After frisking frantically and then going into strange spasms of not breathing at all followed by breathing too fast, they had collapsed upon each other and fallen asleep.

The guard bird, in a show of triumph Aldon suspected it had been waiting a long time for, flew out, barked wildly over their heads, and then flew back to nestle contentedly by his feet.

The plant-men had given up writhing and were now sitting rigidly, rooting as deeply as they could. Something about the aphids was making them less men and more rose-bush.

Despite the wild success of his half of the mission, Aldon was nervous. He'd heard Tereska's war whoop and seen Umbria go after her just as they'd planned, but after that nothing had happened—except for an odd rumbling that sounded like someone very deep-voiced and terrible was speaking in the halls above.

And now he had a feeling that something had gone wrong. Brig had been laying still, but now he was shaking. Aldon laid his hand on the sheepdog's head. Brig whined.

The north tower, highest and most prominent of the palace's spires, swayed like a daisy in a breeze. There was no breeze. Nor had the north tower ever acted particularly like a daisy before. Aldon saw it swaying and glued his eyes to it. Something very bad was about to happen.

The guard bird lifted into the air, squawking and barking and carrying on until Brig hid his nose under his paws for shame.

Windows on opposite ends of the tower shattered at the same time, and out from them two black leathery wingtips appeared. A moment later the entire top of the tower gave way in a burst that sent brick and whitewashed stone and glass showering all over the walls and the courtyard. Out of the hole a great black terror appeared.

It was the dragon, and Ignus Umbria was seated on its neck, looking much like a parasite enjoying the dark glory of its host. For a moment they floated in the air, suspended against the sky, and the air seemed to grow suddenly darker even as the smell of sulfur and smoke filled it. Then they descended, not flapping down like the guard bird which squawked down beneath them and frantically dove for a hiding place in the eaves of the palace, but gracefully riding the air currents like a feather that drifts to the ground.

Only this feather was deadly.

Aldon stayed frozen in place. He knew he ought to do something: to get up, to run, to bolt for cover. But the part of him capable of thinking in that moment was not sure there was any real cover to be had. The dragon had just burst its way through a roof. The man riding it was an evil genius. Worst of all, their plan had failed, and Aldon had no guarantees that he and Brig were not the last of the gallant revolution.

Umbria unwittingly gave Aldon cause to take heart as soon as he opened his mouth. His whole tone of voice was triumphant, almost laughing. The mad magician was in his element: showing a degree of his power that had never been seen before, and showing it to his only openly declared enemies—most of whom Aldon could only assume were still alive. The speech was a little too grandiose to be addressed merely to a boy and a sheepdog.

"Hear me, invaders!" he called out. His voice was the only sound to be heard. Even the guard bird had fallen completely silent, trembling as it was in a crook of stone above Aldon. "You thought you could challenge me? Well, I accept your challenge! Invade my sanctum! Turn my weapons against me, if you can! But I will not hold anything back."

Umbria looked down. His glittering eyes fixed themselves on Aldon. "Don't think I don't see you," he said. His voice was still loud enough to carry throughout the courtyard, and from there to the others who were listening in their various places. "I count each of you as my enemies, and I will defeat every last one of you."

Then he grinned. It was a nasty grin. "Do what you can to save yourselves, but do not think you can simply run away and come back another time when I'm not expecting you. I have magicked the walls against you. There is no way out except through me."

With those words he raised his right hand and shouted in a voice that seemed to shake the foundations of the palace—but with noise, not with the latent power Tomas had earlier displayed—"Minions! Gather to me!"

He pointed his finger at a bush in a garden before him. A burst of lightning jumped from its tip and lit the bush on fire. The effect on the pyrolines was almost immediate. They stretched themselves, yawning their great jaws and showing piercing teeth. The bigger one, underneath its fellow, clawed at the smaller one, making it jump up and protest. Shaking their heads so that their black manes stood on end, they slunk toward the fire and began to roll in it, with the slow, lazy roll of a cat who has just awakened from sleep and is stretching itself. Even as they did, Aldon caught a nervous glimpse of the plant-men. They were moving—uprooting themselves very slowly.

Umbria seemed to grow tired of waiting for them. This time he aimed both hands at the spurting fountain. Such a bolt jumped from his palms that it shattered the fountain in pieces, and a geyser exploded out of the ground and rained down on the length of the courtyard. Even with the stone wall and the roof overhead, Aldon got a good dousing. Worse, the plant-men did. Aldon watched in horror as the water seemed to give them strength. They pulled themselves out of the ground and crawled toward the thickest showers, where the aphids were washed away by the flow.

They came out the other side visibly stronger. They shook themselves with the damp sound of leaves slapping against each other in the wind. Aldon could see holes in their layers where the aphids had eaten through, but after all, what were a few holes to a plant? Their woody arms and legs seemed damaged in places, but still strong enough to do a great deal of capturing, crushing, and beating.

Then they turned their cabbage-rose-like heads, fixed their grey eyes on Aldon, and moved forward. He jumped to his feet even as Brig growled and looked frantically for some place to run.

High in the wreckage of the north tower, Celine pulled herself out from a heap of rubble that had managed to fall in just such a way that it trapped but did not crush her. The Machine, she noticed as she climbed over part of it, was still whole. Her uncle was a fine craftsman, this she had to admit. What he built stood up to abuse. Even to the abuse of having a roof and pieces of wall fall on it.

She crawled across the floor, searching intently through the rubble. "Winnie!" she called, her voice sharp with worry. She cleared her throat—lime whitewash made her raspy. "Winnie!"

A pile of crumbled stone moved not far away. Celine lurched forward and whisked the white dust away, uncovering a trembling wombat that appeared as whitewashed as the walls had been. "Winnie!" she said, relieved this time. Beady black eyes blinked up at her.

"What happened?"

"The ceiling fell," Celine said. "My uncle . . . Winnie, let's get out of here. We have to stop him!"

So saying, she scrambled to her feet, half-walked, half-jumped over the large bits of wall in her way, and flung the door open.

Malic was standing on the other side. His sword was drawn, his face was florid, and his eyes were vengeful.

"Greetings, my lady," he growled.

In the hall, Tomas, Tereska, Monk, and Sir Brian had all heard every word of Umbria's challenge. For a moment they stood frozen. Sir Brian held his battle-axe a little higher, and Tomas turned a determined shade of pale. The anger and hatred that had so lately overwhelmed him had left him exhausted, and back of it all there was still grief—was still a heart very much broken. He did not feel like battling Umbria. In fact, if he'd ever wished himself far away from his destiny, it was now. But that did not change the fact that these others were here, and they needed him, and after all, if someone was going to save the day, it seemed logical that an Immortal should do it.

Tereska also turned pale, also with determination. She was fairly certain that her ship had sunk. But there was no point in giving up fighting. Monk did not turn anything at all. He forced his chin to stop quivering and hold heroically still. The little pyroline meowed.

"Is he still here?" Sir Brian exclaimed, breaking their silence with his booming voice. "Curse that little man! I thought I'd been frozen there for lifetimes."

"You likely were," Tereska said. "Umbria's Immortal."

Sir Brian looked at Tomas, then back out the window at the black dragon and Umbria seated on its neck. As he watched, the fountain burst forth and the plant-men began to drag themselves through the cleansing showers. "Too many Immortals, if you ask me," Sir Brian said.

"What are we going to do?" Tereska asked. Her voice was tight.

"Your plan," Tomas said. "Your old plan. We're still going to do it. Use his weapons against him, as he said. Where's the north tower?"

"North," Tereska answered. Then she burst out, "He destroyed the north tower!"

"No," Tomas said. "He wouldn't just destroy his own work. If he created that Machine, it's still there. The tower hasn't come down completely—only the roof fell in. Er, out."

Tereska pointed down the long corridor. "It's that way."

Celine looked around her as she backed slowly away. Malic came through the door, stumbling over bits of the walls. He was still brandishing his sword.

Celine spied a bit of twisted metal half-buried in dust: a girder from the ceiling. She snatched it up and held it as a defense, thanking God that it had come loose without trouble. Malic laughed at her. "Going to face off with that, are you?" he asked.

He cut a blow with his sword. Celine moved quickly enough to deflect it, but the impact was so strong that she nearly dropped the girder. Malic was many things. Weak was not one of them.

He lifted his sword and swung it again. Again she caught it, but this time the blow vibrated through her sore shoulder, and she winced.

Malic laughed. He took a step closer. "We thought you were dead," he said. "That boy almost blew up with rage when he heard it. Too bad Umbria's going to get him . . . you'd have made such a lovely couple." His voice suddenly turned dark. "But I want my vengeance. If I can't have him, I'll have you!"

And he raised his sword to deal a blow that would cut right through Celine's girder and leave her helpless. Only the blow never fell. Instead, Malic's eyes grew wide, and he howled with pain.

Winnie had fastened all ten claws in his leg and bitten him behind the knee with every ounce of rodentlike jaw power she could muster. Malic's leg buckled, and he dropped to one knee. Winnie just managed to let go and jump aside in time.

Celine saw her moment. She swung back with the girder and brought it around and against the side of Malic's head as hard as she could. His eyes rolled back, and he fell forward. Celine jumped over him. Winnie scurried close to her heels, and the pair of them left the north tower and ran.

The plant-men reached Aldon and surrounded him. Brig launched himself at them, barking and gnashing his teeth, but one of the plant-men grabbed him by the tail, lifted him off the ground, and threw him against a wall. Aldon scrambled to run, but he slipped on the wet flagstones. A strong woody hand grabbed his ankle and hauled him off the ground. He found himself dangling, his head only inches from the stone. Water streamed from his hair and clothing.

A pair of boots approached and stopped before him.

"One down," Umbria said in a voice too unpleasant for words. "That was far too easy."

Aldon spit, ridding himself of the nasty taste of fountain water. "Let me go," he said. "I'll make it harder next time."

"I would," Umbria agreed, "but hostages are so good for leverage, don't you think?"

Umbria crouched so that he could look into Aldon's face. The boy was quickly turning red from being held upside down. "I know you," Umbria said. "My shepherd, turned traitor." He tsked. "One of my sheep went missing last week. Do you know where it is?"

"Your dragon ate it," Aldon answered in a strangled voice. "Wandered away so I couldn't put it in the sheepfold."

"Hmm," Umbria said. "I'll have to talk to the dragon about whose livestock he picks off. The aphids were very clever. Did you think that up yourself?"

Aldon thought of Tereska but said nothing. He had a feeling that the less information Umbria was given, the better. The man was far too good at using knowledge.

"The catnip was also clever, but not quite so effective," Umbria continued. "It wears off. Didn't you know that? And once it does, it's hours and hours before the cats are affected again. If, for example, I was to throw you to the pyrolines right now, they would just eat you. All that powder you've rubbed behind your ears wouldn't do you a lick of good."

Aldon flushed, which, considering that he was already turning an unnatural shade, made him look redder than your average tomato—and quite a bit more vulnerable. Behind him, he felt something hot draw near, and then heard the terrifying low purring noise of a pyroline looking over its dinner with pleasure.

But Umbria looked up at the pyroline that was waiting just behind the plant-men and scowled. "No," he said. "I'm not feeding you yet. None of your fat sloth until you've served me well. There are others to catch."

The dragon hissed.

Umbria looked over his shoulder and stared at the black, serpentine face for a moment. "Not you either," he said. He straightened up and barked orders at the plant-men. "Drop the boy. Bind him. Bring him along. We'll gather all the little players before putting an end to this game."

The plant-men obeyed. Aldon landed on his head with a protest, but his vision had no time to stop spinning before the plant-men had pulled him to his feet and tied his arms and feet with corded vines. Two of them hefted him between them as though he were a piece of wood. Behind him, Brig yelped as the plant-men tied his feet together and one of them slung him over his shoulder.

Umbria marched ahead of them like a cannibal king heading up a band of hungry natives and their captives. He climbed ungracefully back onto the dragon's back, took up his reins, and said, with a piercing look at his followers, "To the Great Hall. We make our stand there." His small eyes glittered, and he smiled that nasty smile again. "Quickly may they come."

Chapter 15

WINNIE'S HEART WAS BEATING FASTER than any human heart would ever go, and as Celine was holding her tucked close, she could feel every beat. Her own heart wasn't going much slower. Her blow had taken Malic out for a moment, but she didn't expect the moment to be a long one. Confronting Malic had felt to her much like facing the dreaded pyrolines. Her uncle was a wretch, and more unpredictable than she'd thought him, but he was familiar. Malic was something alien, and he hated her.

That knowledge shook her almost as much as Tomas's love had threatened to do before she got too busy to think about it.

Winnie's voice was breathless and muffled by the cloth of Celine's dress. "Where are we going?"

Celine reached a cross-corridor and looked around her, choosing one at random and running down it. She passed a suit of armour and stopped to borrow its sword, though she disliked the weight and feel of the thing, and its tip wanted to drag on the ground and trip her up. "Here," she explained.

Through the corridor, Tomas, Tereska, and Sir Brian ran. Had they stopped to look five feet down the hall, they would have seen Celine—but they didn't. Nor did she look back and see them.

Winnie's voice was beginning to calm a little. "How are we going to stop him, Celine?"

"I'm not sure," Celine said, resolutely dragging the sword behind her. She had stopped running. Winnie's questions had highlighted the fact that she didn't know just where she was going, so she was in no great hurry to get there. If Malic was behind her, hopefully he'd lost himself in the maze of luxuriously decorated hallways.

She stopped. "I suppose we should find the others."

"What others?" Winnie asked.

"Whoever else is here. Whoever my uncle is so hell-bent on finding."

Winnie scratched her ear. "Why?"

"Maybe they'll have good ideas," Celine said.

"They thought breaking in here was a good idea," Winnie pointed out.

"Well," Celine said, "we can always hope."

She attempted to heft the sword, but it was heavy, and she took a step backwards—right into a golden suit of armour.

"Hey!" the suit of armour burst out. "Watch where you're going!"

A clanking noise from the end of the hallway called for Celine's attention. She looked away from the talking suit to see another one making its stiff-legged way toward her. This suit was grey, and it lifted an iron-plated finger and pointed straight at her.

"That's my sword!" it said.

Tomas led the way to the north tower. He was driven by a sheer sense of duty. *Have to do this. Have to help Aldon. Have to get Tereska out. Have to save Monk. Have to be a worthy ally to this Sir Brian fellow, whatever he was about. Have to—finally have to—defeat Umbria like he'd been born to do.*

It was with this rhythm of "have to" beating in his head and through his limbs, pulling his broken heart behind him, that he nearly ran headlong into Malic.

"You again!" he said.

Malic was an ugly shade of purple. The side of his head looked slightly dented. His sword was drawn.

"Where is she?" he bellowed.

Tomas's heart quirked in a queer little fashion that was painful but good, because it was reminding him that it was still there.

"Who?" Tomas asked.

"That cursed wench you're here to save!" Malic answered. He was peering over Tomas's shoulder and around his thin form, looking as though he would burst through them all like a bowling ball through five pins if he could catch a glimpse of his prey.

Tomas's voice shook. Never in his life had it done so before, but that didn't seem to matter now. "You said she was dead," Tomas said.

"So I did!" Malic roared. "Now I'm telling you different. It wasn't a ghost bashed my head now, was it? Wasn't a ghost hound that bit me in the leg." Malic gnashed his teeth. It was unbecoming.

"She's alive?" Tomas asked. Malic didn't have to answer. All of a sudden, the broken pieces of Tomas's heart bounded back together. He nearly jumped for the joy of it. "She's alive!" he shouted. He turned around, grabbed Tereska's hands, and danced her in a circle. "She's alive!"

"Yes, you fool!" Tereska snapped. "And so's that—" She intended to warn Tomas that Malic had seen an opportunity and was about to cleave him in two with his sword, but Sir Brian saw the danger first and crossed swords with the ruffian.

"On guard!" Sir Brian said. The big man in black armour made Malic look like a dwarf. Malic shrank back.

"Let me by," he said. "I won't bother you anymore."

Sir Brian was about to ask Tomas what to do, but Tomas was in no mood to put anyone out of commission. He was already headed back toward the north tower, putting Malic entirely behind him. The beat in his head and heart and limbs had changed. No more "have to." Now every pulse said "She's alive!"

Tereska and Sir Brian looked at one another. Sir Brian shrugged and started to let down his sword, which was still crossed with Malic's.

"No," Tereska said. "We can't just let him go."

"Very well," Sir Brian said, seeming to brighten. "We'll finish him off."

Tomas's skinny form was still drawing farther away. He seemed unaware that anything was happening behind him. Tereska sighed deep within her. She was not entirely devoid of pity, and Malic was beginning to look worthy of it. His purple face had gone grey. He had realized he was facing death at the hands of the giant in black armour, and he was not one to face it very gracefully.

Then something very unexpected happened. Monk cleared his throat and said, "No. We should release him. It is right."

Tereska looked at the old, old man in surprise. He looked somehow straighter—nobler. The pyroline was holding its orange-and-grey head high, ear tufts sticking straight up.

"Let him go to his master," Monk said. "He has chosen him. Let each side rally together and stand or fall together."

He blinked his watery eyes. His voice was a little less assured as he finished, "It seems . . . right to me."

Sir Brian lowered his sword suddenly. He grabbed Malic by the scruff of the neck and tossed him down the hall. He nodded to Monk approvingly. "There is honour in you, old man," he said. "We shall do as you say."

And so a very lucky Malic scrambled yet again to his feet and ran to his master—to Umbria, whom, until that moment, he would never have acknowledged as master. But he had thrown his lot into another man's fortunes whether he knew it or not, and the time was now to pay the consequences.

Tereska, Sir Brian, and Monk looked back to the end of the hall where Tomas had disappeared.

"Stand together," Tereska said. "You're right. That's what we should do. But that means we need to go into the court-yard."

"I don't understand," Monk said.

"Aldon's down there," Tereska explained. "We let him be captured without even trying to help."

"The girl is out there somewhere too," Sir Brian said. "The one the Immortal lad seeks."

The pyroline mewed. "And," Monk said, "whatever bit Malic in the leg."

Tereska crossed the hall and disappeared into a small, dark room. The others joined her. A window looked down on the courtyard. The dragon, with Umbria on its neck, held throne in the very middle of the flagstones. The pyrolines prowled around them. The plant-men were arrayed like a living wall, facing outward. Behind them, at the base of the shattered spurting fountain, Aldon and Brig sat tied up like chickens.

Apparently no one was paying much attention to them, because Aldon was holding out his bound hands, and a large white bird was pecking the vines free. Tereska cheered under her breath. Now . . . how to get Aldon out once he was free?

Her thoughts were interrupted by a loud noise in the hallway: a crash, a yelp, and a muffled shout.

It sounded like a suit of armour tripping over something.

Tomas was still singing "She's alive" to himself when he reached the north tower. One look assured him that the Machine was still intact and operable. And also hopelessly confusing. Umbria, with his love of science, magic, and craftsmanship, had not put much effort into making his work accessible to laymen—even if the layman in question was Immortal.

The controls were laid out on a panel beside the Machine. They could be operated from without, if one was trying to send someone away, or from within, if one had a desire to travel. The Machine itself was elegantly designed. It consisted of a round golden rim on the floor, which normally gleamed but was now dulled by bits of wall and roof and powdered lime dust. Over this, a slender arm reached. At the end of the arm was an oval disc about the same diameter as three human heads.

Tomas was not sure how to operate the controls, but neither was he particularly afraid of anything—not now that Celine was alive. So he made sure he was well outside of the rim and then began to push buttons. The whole control panel lit up as he did, and a dizzying series of images appeared as he touched the buttons. They moved so fast that he hardly had time to register the first image as that of a great cavern with a hearth, where bones littered the floor and a distinct aura of dragon lingered. He wondered who'd been lately sent there and guessed it was Umbria . . . likely he had brought the dragon back into the tower.

He kept fiddling with the buttons until one image came into view and stayed there, glowing red and alien and promising.

Tereska and Sir Brian looked at one another. "My men!" Sir Brian said, and ran from the little room. Tereska followed. Monk looked down at the pyroline, said, "They never hold still, do they?" and followed after them.

They ran down the corridor, turned left, and came upon Celine with a furry grey creature trembling on her shoulder. There was a suit of armour threatening her before and behind. One was golden, gleaming, and newly dented in the shoulder; the other was grey. Neither had removed his helmet, so both retained the eerie impression of being pieces of hall decoration that had sprung bizarrely to life.

Sir Brian took in the situation at a glance and roared, "Fall in!"

The suits of armour clanked to a halt. The one facing Celine turned around as gracefully as ever a tin can could. Both took one look at Sir Brian and fell, noisily, to one knee.

"My lord!" the golden suit said.

"Remove your helmet," Sir Brian said. The golden suit did so. The head underneath it was large, hairy, and blonde. Confused puddle-brown eyes looked up at Sir Brian.

"Helmut," Sir Brian said. "Welcome back to life, brother."

"Yes, my lord," Helmut said. "I am pleased to be alive, my lord. But, my lord, I am confused."

"Me too," clanked the grey suit.

"Remove your helmet," Sir Brian said, sounding displeased.

"I would, my lord," said the grey suit. "But I think it's rusted on."

"Very well," Sir Brian said. "Rise, both of you, and draw your swords."

The grey suit pointed at Celine. "She's got mine."

Celine was standing rigidly in the center of all this, not even wincing as Winnie dug her claws into her shoulder. She had drawn the sword and was holding it so tightly that her knuckles had turned white.

"Who are you?" she demanded. "What's going on?" A meow pulled her eyes past Sir Brian. "Grandfather Monk!" she cried.

"Hello, dear child," Monk said.

Tereska had taken in as much of the situation as she could. "We're with Tomas," she said. "You're Celine."

"Yes," Celine said. "Do I know you?"

"Not really," Tereska said. "I scrubbed floors before you did."

"Oh," Celine said.

"We're here to revolt against your uncle, but things have gone badly. Tomas is in the north tower," Tereska said. "This is Sir Brian. He's a suit of armour. Or he was. But he's on our side, so I think these other two are too."

"Good," Celine said. She was still gripping the sword.

"You can give that one back his sword," Tereska said, nodding at the bereft suit of armour. "Chances are he can lift it better than you can."

Celine turned and looked at the grey suit. "You're on our side?" she said. "Word of honour?"

The grey suit looked at Sir Brian, who nodded. "Word

of honour," the suit promised.

"You'll not threaten us again?" Celine said. There was a gleam of mischief in her eye. She was not happy with the erstwhile suits, and she suspected that threatening a lady would get them in trouble with Sir Brian. As she thought, both Helmut and the grey suit turned to Sir Brian to protest.

"She stole my sword!" said the grey suit.

"And attacked me," Helmut added.

"Nothing of the kind," Celine said, nose in the air. "He tripped over my wombat."

Sir Brian glared at his knights. "I'm not pleased with the manner in which I found you," he said. "But now is hardly the time for recrimination."

The men halted mid-sigh of relief when Sir Brian added, "We'll do that later. My lady, kindly rearm my knight."

Celine handed over the sword. The grey suit of armour took it with relish and hefted it several times, ignoring the slight tinge of rust on the blade—and even the threat of Sir Brian's censure—for the sheer glory of being alive and armed again.

Grandfather Monk toddled across the hall floor with a determined air, quietly bent on protecting his princess. Celine kissed his forehead and looked down at the pyroline twining around her ankles—which behaviour was making Winnie nervous. "Don't dig so hard, Winnie," she said. Then to the pyroline, "It's even good to see you again."

She turned back to Tereska and said, "Tomas is in the

north tower? Why? My uncle destroyed it with that dragon of his!"

"Was the Machine destroyed?" Tereska asked.

Celine hesitated. "No."

"Tomas wants to use it, then," Tereska said. "It's been our plan all along—Aldon's and mine. To send Umbria to some far-off country where he'll have to leave us alone."

"He sent me to the moon," Celine said. "Who's Aldon?"

"The shepherd," Tereska said. "He's the other half of the revolution—well, half and a quarter, with that dog of his—and Umbria's got him trussed up in the courtyard."

"Oh," Celine said. "I need to see Tomas."

Tereska gave her a look of disgust, one laden with words like "lovesick hen," but said nothing other than, "Well, we need to regroup. And we have no group till we get Aldon away. As long as Umbria's got a hostage he'll wait for us to come to him."

"We can't get Aldon away *without* going to him," Celine pointed out.

Tereska folded her pencil-thin, rag-wrapped arms and looked at Sir Brian.

"All you have to do," she said in a tone of utmost reason, "is charge in there, bowl the plant-men aside, throw Aldon and Brig over your shoulders, and run back out before Umbria catches you. If he follows, head for the north tower. That's where we want him. Tomas will have the Machine ready."

Sir Brian opened his mouth, but no words came out. In their place, a chivalrous gleam leaped into his eye. "My lady!" he said, dropping a deep bow.

Tereska's eyebrow twitched. "Would you *not* call me that?"

"When Umbria spelled the lot of us for revolting against him—somewhere else—I heard the spell. Only the touch of a lady could break it."

Celine and Winnie exchanged a glance. That explained a few things. It was nice to know that Winnie, backing up into a suit of armour with enough force to knock it over, still qualified as a lady.

"Irrelevant," Tereska snapped, even though it wasn't. She lifted a skinny arm and pointed toward the courtyard. "Charge!"

The guard bird had pecked the vines clear away from Aldon's hands and feet. When the last tendril snapped free, Aldon rolled over and untied Brig. The poor dog was still in pain from being thrown against the wall, and Aldon had to work hard not to show how anxious he was or call attention to himself by talking to the dog.

When Brig was loose—though not very responsive—Aldon got onto his hands and knees and crawled very slowly away from the base of the fountain toward the wall of plant-men. He blessed the unnatural darkness that had fallen when the dragon appeared; it kept him from being noticed.

When he was close enough to smell the peculiar spicy smell of the plant-men and to reach out, if he wanted to, and tweak their heels, he stopped. Where to go from here was a problem. The creatures were not especially bowlegged, but he perhaps *could* crawl through the legs of the one standing nearest him. If he did he would certainly call attention to himself, and then he'd have to get to his feet and sprint all the way across the courtyard and through a door to safety, and of course the whole lot of them would probably be right behind him by then if they hadn't caught him already.

He let his legs go flat on the ground and rested his chin in his hand. His whole face was scrunched in a frown.

And then the door directly across the courtyard—a high purple one—burst open, and a pair of ironclad legs beat their way toward him while a baritone voice hollered something eloquent but much too hollered to be clearly understood. At exactly the same time, the two doors next to the purple one also burst open, and two more ironclad pairs of legs rushed toward the plant-men.

Aldon was not one to miss a chance. He scrambled back onto his knees and all but catapulted himself forward. His head went right through the plant-man's legs. His stocky shoulders hit the creature's knees with enough force to buckle them. The plant-man came down on top of him, but with a mighty heave Aldon threw him off, got to his feet, and started running—then tripped on a cobblestone and sprawled out on the ground.

As he tried to push himself back up, he heard the voice of Ignus Umbria shout something. Off to the left, a golden charging suit of armour disappeared.

In its place was a large golden cricket.

On Aldon's right, a grey suit of armour skidded to a halt and looked around for some cover. It didn't do a bit of good. Umbria shouted again, and another cricket hopped across the flagstones. Aldon pushed himself onto his palms. The first suit of armour he had seen, a big black one, was still coming. Aldon looked behind him and saw Umbria lower his hand and open his mouth to shout, pointing at the black suit. Aldon hit the ground again as a bolt of energy flew over him . . . and missed. The black suit of armour had thrown itself aside just in time.

Aldon got back up and ran for the purple door. Another bolt of energy flew past him with another shout. It missed again. The black suit was running zigzags across the court-yard, more nimble and quick than any man wearing so much weight should ever be.

The black suit passed Aldon in the courtyard, and a deep voice boomed, "Run!" Aldon was already obeying. The black suit jumped a foot in the air as a bolt of energy hit the ground directly beneath it. When it hit the flagstones again, it was still running.

Sir Brian drew his sword in one hand and wielded his battle-axe in the other. He charged into the line of plant-men yelling like an enraged buffalo. Vegetable matter flew on every side of him. With a hardly discernible pause, he threw Brig over his shoulder and turned to go.

But he could not resist stopping, peering over his shoulder, and looking into the eyes of Umbria and his dragon.

"We're free at last," he bellowed.

Umbria raised his hand to fire yet another bolt of transformative energy. Just then another voice sounded out over the courtyard. It was Tomas's.

He was standing on the ruined wall of the north tower, outlined against the sky like a tall, spindly star. His wild hair seemed to shine. His eyes were blazing with life. Even at such a distance, his presence could be felt.

"Umbria!" he called with a voice almost joyful. "Come and face me!"

Ignus Umbria's attention was pulled entirely away from Sir Brian. He had not expected to see Tomas in the north tower or looking so happy. It made no earthly sense to him that Tomas *should* be happy—wasn't Celine still dead? In fact, Tomas's happiness almost made him angry. But Tomas was standing very prominently in a very high place, and it was a clear shot, and there was the spell still boiling away in his hand, waiting to be released at someone.

So Ignus Umbria turned away from Sir Brian and prepared to throw his spell at the scarecrow of an Immortal who had at last come to challenge him.

And then the dragon changed everything. Without Umbria's direction or desire, it opened its mouth and let out a burst of fire.

Chapter 16

CELINE SAW THE DRAGON OPEN ITS MOUTH, jerk its head back, and let out a stream of flame. She was watching at a window that looked over the courtyard. Her eyes grew wide, and she opened her mouth to warn the others to run. But before she could, the heat of the blast shattered the window pane on which she was leaning, and she pitched forward.

There was a flagpole just below the window, and she grabbed it and dangled from it, and Winnie, who had been on her shoulder, fell down to the courtyard.

The flame was licking up some fuel between the flagstones (catnip and water, truth be told, which had hardened into a paste—not that such a fuel would have been especially attractive to just any fire, but this one wasn't ordinary), slicing off whole sections of the courtyard from each other. Sir

Brian stood in one large rectangular space near the dragon's feet, with Brig still over his shoulder and the guard bird barking in the air over him. Across a high-burning, thin wall of flame, Aldon stood frozen with shock near the purple door. And next to him, behind yet another wall of flame, Winnie was trapped against the wall. The fire was just beneath Celine and licking almost at her feet, but though it was hot it did not actually reach her.

"Winnie!" Celine cried. And then she changed her tune. "Aldon! Aldon, rescue Winnie!"

Aldon took in the situation fairly quickly. He looked through the tongues of flame and saw the little grey creature huddled against the wall, and he looked up at the princess whose life was held in balance by a flagpole. He looked down at his still-wet clothes, and then at the purple door which awaited him.

"Why should I risk my neck for a rodent?" Aldon asked incredulously.

Celine was about to retort that hadn't a bird's pecking saved *his* life, and shouldn't he be a little less picky about species? but then, the bird wasn't really a bird. Neither, Celine realized with a flash of inspiration, was Winnie really a wombat.

"She's not a rodent!" Celine called. Whether Aldon made those words out or not she wasn't sure, but he did hear the next part. "She's a girl!" Celine yelled. "A beautiful girl! Save the girl!"

Aldon huffed, sputtered, grumbled, pulled his shirt up

so it partially covered his head, and charged through the thin wall of fire. He came out the other side smoldering, grabbed Winnie, tucked her under his shirt, and ran back through. The tail of his shirt caught fire when he came out the other side, and he threw Winnie toward the door, hit the ground, and rolled. The fire went out, leaving a black stain.

Aldon jumped up, grasped the handle of the purple door, and pulled. Nothing happened. He pulled again, harder, jerking the door now. It wouldn't come loose. He turned and looked wildly back through the flames at Umbria. He'd locked it somehow.

And then, even as he tugged, he smelled burning cotton and felt heat behind him. The shirt had rekindled. Not pausing to think how it had managed to do so, water-saturated though it was, Aldon tore the whole shirt off and threw it into the fire.

Hoisted as far up on the flagpole as she could manage, Celine watched in horror as the fire rekindled. No one else heard the words that escaped her lips.

"Ravening Fire."

Then Celine heard a sound: a deep, unnerving, even terrifying sound. It was the sound of purring when purring is evil and hungry. She looked down.

The pyrolines were circling beneath her.

Tomas saw the fire kindle from his post high on the north tower, and he knew exactly what it was. The dragon had only to open its mouth and let forth the flame, and he knew.

Umbria had not found the dragon somewhere. He had created it. All of his experiments in turning one thing into another thing had led to the great, black, scaly beast below: Umbria's masterpiece. And there was a more terrifying truth still.

It breathed Ravening Fire.

Suddenly, Tomas Solandis understood why it was necessary that he be born. For the first time in his life he knew that Umbria had to be defeated—that it was not a question of maybe, or if, or of whether Umbria pushed things too far or not. Ignus Umbria's insatiable lust for new power was enough to devour the whole world, and it would do exactly that. Tomas also understood in that moment the terrible consequences of procrastination. There was indeed a proper time to defeat Ignus Umbria, and that time was, and had always been, as soon as possible.

Tomas looked down on a courtyard with flames licking up between blocks of flagstones, creating a checkerboard on which various souls were trapped. He saw Sir Brian, the noble knight, near the dragon's feet with Brig, the noble dog, over his shoulder. He saw Aldon and Winnie unable to get through the door into the palace and cut off by the fire from finding any other door. He saw Umbria in the center of it all, high above the flames on the black dragon's neck.

Tomas knew Ravening Fire. He knew that this one would burn beyond the normal power of flame. The longer it burned the stronger it would grow, until it began to eat up even the flagstones and foundations of the palace. He knew that it would spread, then, because while Ravening Fire could sometimes be captured and contained, this one was too big—and besides, it lived in the belly of a dragon that would surely kindle it again. When it spread it would turn the hillside and forest to ash, and then eat the town and all its inhabitants, and from there it would go on to set the sea ablaze, and all the world. Ignus Umbria might, like tyrants of old, fiddle and sing at the work of his hands, but eventually it would get him too—he and the monster he had created.

In short, as Tomas looked down on the courtyard he knew there was no hope. Not for him, not for the revolution, not for the entire world.

And then he spotted Celine, clinging to a flagpole with flames and the pyrolines, the sole creatures not affected by the outbreak of fire, threatening her.

And at the sight his heart gave a little leap and sang, "She's alive!"

He turned and looked behind him at the Machine that still stood under its powdering of shattered roof. Far below, he heard the voice of a genius laughing.

Suddenly, there was hope again.

Chapter 17

SMOKE ROSE AROUND CELINE. It made the flagpole grimy and slick beneath her fingers, along with sweat from her hands, but she clutched it with hands and knees and prayed for deliverance. Her heart was palpitating, and she shut her eyes to make it stop. The pyrolines—oh, curse the pyrolines and the fear they inspired! She was glad Winnie had gotten away—she'd likely be burned alive but that was better than being eaten by pyrolines—glad to have seen Tomas standing on the tower one last time—glad to have at least tried to battle Umbria before he went farther than she'd ever thought he would and won the whole world by losing it.

She wondered if pyrolines would still be able to live in a world that had been entirely Ravened. She doubted it. The fire would keep burning until the world was the size of child's ball, and the pyrolines would fall off.

She looked up at the dark window she'd fallen through, desperate for a hand to reach down to her. It would be so unaccountably nice if Tomas would suddenly appear on the other side.

She was beginning to tremble from the effort of holding on. Smoke stung her eyes. It would be nice, she thought again, despite the niggling fear that such thoughts were futile. When one only had an another hour or so to live, one appreciated hope.

Aldon had ceased trying to figure out why the purple door wouldn't open and had begun alternately pounding on it with his fists and hurling his entire body into it. What the wombat was doing he did not know and did not stop to figure out—beautiful girl or no beautiful girl, he didn't expect her to be of much use.

On the other side of the door, Tereska was pulling at the handle with all of her skinny might. Unsuccessful, she stopped once and pounded on its purple oak with her own fist. Grandfather Monk appeared confused by this, but he stepped forth and said, "Stand back, my dear."

Tereska did. Her eyes were tearful and her hands nearly pulled apart from trying to open the unaccountably locked door. Aldon threw himself against it once more, but the wood didn't even quake at the blow. Monk lifted his broomstick and tried to wedge its end between the door and its frame. It did no good.

Outside, Aldon drew back for another run when the wombat's voice halted him in his tracks.

"This way!" she called.

He stopped in mid-draw and looked at her. She was standing in a pile of dirt, quivering with excitement. She'd been digging, and he saw that the hole was just big enough for him to squirm his way through.

"No!" he said. "Ye'll not trap me underground!"

"It's no trap!" Winnie said. She scratched her ear almost frantically. "It's a way out!"

Aldon looked up at the wall of flame that hemmed them in. It was orange and alive. He looked back at the stalwart purple of the door and then down at the heap of dirt. Winnie gave him a scathing glance with her black eyes and then disappeared headfirst down the hole.

Tereska stared at Grandfather Monk as he tried again to somehow get the broomstick into place where it could act as a lever. The little pyroline was making agitated circles near his feet. The few moments she'd been replaced at the door had given her time to think. She reached into her cloak and pulled out a sword in a white sheath. Grandfather Monk's eyes grew large.

"Where did you get that?" he asked, pointing a shaking finger.

"Stole it from Umbria," Tereska said. With a light, fluid motion, she drew the sword from its sheath. The words at the base of the blade were glowing: *Umbria's Bane.*

"Stand away," Tereska said. As Monk obeyed, she lifted the sword and brought it down, cleaving a neat path between the door and its frame. It was like slicing through an invisible seal, and through the now-enlarged crack, flame could be seen. With a shout of triumph, Tereska cast the sword aside and pulled the door open.

It swung open easily, but Aldon was nowhere to be seen.

Tereska blinked at the empty square, surrounded by flames. The little pyroline shot between her feet, straight into the fire. She hardly noticed. She took a step after it, almost startled by the heat in the air. The flames were drawing closer, making the air waver. She squinted.

A pile of dirt marked the hole where Aldon must have disappeared.

Before she could think what to do, a baritone voice called "Ho!" and held the note for a long time. Before her unbelieving eyes, Sir Brian sailed over the wall of flames and landed, with a loud crack on the flagstones, directly before her. On his shoulders and head were arrayed a dog and two large crickets. He bowed, dislodging the top cricket.

"My lady," he said.

She had no time to protest before a very bad thing happened.

Overhead, the flames jumped. They went from the wall

in the flagstone cracks to a banner just above them, sending down sparks that lit the purple door on fire. Tereska's eyes widened, and she turned and bolted back inside. Without stopping—hardly even slowing down—she picked up the sword, hooked her arm with Grandfather Monk's, and raced away from the advancing flames. Sir Brian's ironclad foot-steps struck the ground behind her.

Aldon crawled on his hands and knees through the dark earth. It was cool below the courtyard, as though the raging fire above existed in some entirely other world. After the initial drop through dirt that was soft and crumbling, he found himself crawling on hard-packed earth in a tunnel far larger than he had imagined.

"Where are ye taking me?" he asked. He almost said "rodent," but bit his tongue. Glad to be underground he was not, but he was away from the flames, and the grey creature ahead of him might, after all, not always be a rodent. The knowledge that he and the wombat now owed each other their lives was slightly disconcerting, but he took comfort in the words Celine had shouted.

"It's my burrow," the wombat's voice came back. "We're going into the palace . . . to find the others and save Celine."

"How far does it go?" he asked.

"Everywhere," Winnie answered.

They crawled through the dark for long minutes, Winnie moving at a fast trot, Aldon trying not to hit his head or catch his hair on the roots that hung down into the burrow in places. Then the burrow started to move upward, and Aldon thought he heard footsteps overhead. His heart leaped. Tereska! They would be safe!

Light appeared at the end of the tunnel, disappeared for a moment and came again, and Aldon caught a glimpse of Winnie's back legs scrambling out of the hole. Then she yelped.

Aldon popped his head out a moment later, just in time to be grabbed by the scruff of the neck and thrown against the wall by a plant-man with angry grey eyes. Another was holding Winnie, who was struggling with all her might to escape. Standing before them all, with a look on his face that suggested he had been issuing orders, was Malic.

"Back you go," Malic said with an evil grin. He kicked open a door. Before them was the burning courtyard, with a clear path to Umbria and the black dragon.

"Let us go!" Aldon said as the plant-man grabbed his arm and hauled him to his feet. "Ye're doomed along with us—what good is takin' us out there?"

"I was told to go back to my master," Malic said. "And I'm not going without something to prove my worth."

"I'm not good proof!" Aldon protested. He looked wildly around him and saw Winnie trying desperately to twist herself out of the plant-man's hands. "At least," he said, "ye could let the wee creeture go."

Malic's eyes gleamed. "She bit me," he said. "I think I'll keep her. Maybe dragons like to eat little furry things."

He pointed, and the plant-men hauled Aldon outside, with Winnie just behind.

As they passed into the wavering, fire-hot air, Winnie twisted herself just far enough. She dug her teeth into the plant-man's hand and bit hard.

The creature hardly responded. It stumbled slightly and looked down, blinking at the grey thing in its hand. Winnie glared back up at it and took another bite. And another.

The plant-man realized suddenly that it was being eaten, and it dropped Winnie like a hot coal. Malic bellowed with rage and turned to kick her as she scrambled to her feet.

Aldon saw the huge boot drawn back and the red flush in Malic's face. He saw the furry underbelly and the courageous look in Winnie's beady eyes. He knew the blow would kill her.

And he wrenched himself free and tackled Malic as though he had been the purple door and Aldon was determined to go through him.

"Run, rodent!" Aldon shouted.

Winnie reached her feet, clawed at the ground, and disappeared down another hole.

For Aldon, the jig would have been entirely up. He was entangled in a fistfight with Malic and two plant-men, and though the shepherd boy was particularly adept at fistfights, it was not one he was likely to win.

Two things happened to change this, and both announced themselves by barking. The first was the guard bird, which swooped out of the sky and straight into the chief plant-man's head. It buried its beak deep in the cabbagelike sphere, set its feet against the plant-man's neck, and tried to pull itself out. The plant-man itself reeled from this attack and fell face-first on the ground. It was one of the disadvantages of being humanoid that a beak in the back of the head was disorienting.

The second thing was the arrival of Brig on the shoulder of Sir Brian. Winnie, with her uncanny skill at arriving in the wrong place at the wrong time, had actually brought Aldon into an ambush laid for the others. The others had now arrived and seen what was happening in the courtyard. Sir Brian laid Brig on the ground, knocked both Malic and the second plant-man flying, and pulled Aldon to his feet.

Celine watched the pyrolines as they stared up at her with evil, glowing eyes. Their black manes and red eyes pulsed with the energy of smoke and fire. They were at their strongest, their sleekest, their most terrifying. They were in their element. They circled, powerful and gleaming. She tried to quell the fear they inspired, but it was no use. They could take her at any time: at the height of their strength they were capable of leaping for her. She knew it. She saw the largest one begin to wave its tail, and it crouched, all its muscles set to spring. She clenched her teeth so hard they hurt and looked up at the window one last time, hoping—oh, hoping—for deliverance.

But then something happened below. She heard the high-low sound of a cat announcing its presence: calling a challenge. And when she opened her eyes, she saw something else stalking out of the fire.

The creature's orange fur, deep in colour like red flame, was tipped with grey. Its tufted ears were long. Its muscular body rippled with every step it took, like fire bending in a wind. Its eyes were alive, not red like the others, but orange with the living glow of embers. Where it walked, fire blazed in its footprints.

Celine found that she was smiling. There were tears in her eyes as she welcomed the little pyroline, grown now to the size of a lynx and so very glorious, but still too small—much too small—to help her.

Yet it was far more beautiful and wild than the other two. Umbria had made them from small pyrolines, fashioned them in the way of great lions, given them strength that was not dependent on fire. But the fire-cat that emerged now from the furnace of a courtyard was a truly magic thing, born out of nature's mysteries.

The big pyrolines turned to look at the newcomer. The little one hissed. In the next instant all three were in a screaming tangle, around and over each other like wheels spinning within wheels, spitting and clawing and murdering with all the pent-up murder in every cat.

And then the biggest pyroline jumped back. It sides were heaving; blood streamed and smoked from a wound on its shoulder. It shook its black mane, still spitting.

The other of Umbria's cats lay still beneath the little pyroline's claws. The tears that had come into Celine's eyes when she saw the brave creature slipped out now, and she said, "Yes!" A moment later something caught her attention from above. She looked up and almost by instinct caught Tomas's hand.

Up until that moment, Tomas had been sprinting through the hall. He knew what he had to do and was simply looking for an appropriate window from which to do it. He had considered simply leaping from the tower—but that, unfortunately, was too much risk. One did not simply go around flinging oneself off of buildings and into fires when one was needed to save the world.

Celine was his motivation: her name kept singing in the air. She was just one person in an entire world that needed saving, but he would always think of her; it would be nice to have a face like Celine's to think of when he remembered saving the world—assuming, of course, that he survived to remember it.

Celine was also his greatest regret—and Celine, he now saw as he slowed outside one of the rooms on the wall, was hanging over the fire on a flagpole. His romantic nature would not have finished the sentence that way, but there she was, looking not at all like a flag.

Tomas rushed into the room, bent himself nearly into

a triangle peak over the ledge, and reached for her with a surge of joy.

Winnie was very, very uncertain about what to do. She was huddled in the darkness underground, trembling in every pore, partially from fear at the heat that even here could be felt, but more—much, much more—from hunger.

Plant-men, she thought as viciously as she had ever thought anything, tasted good.

And, after all, there were more of them. She was very hungry.

And, after all, this was war. Everyone, even wombats, should do their part in war.

Hunger overcame fear in one tremendous burst, and Winnie hurled herself back up the tunnel in hopes of coming out beneath the feet of a plant-man.

She didn't. Instead, she came up into a burst of magic which Umbria was at that moment flinging at the escaping Sir Brian.

Sir Brian leapt out of the way. Winnie popped up directly where he had been. Sir Brian spun around to see what had happened and found himself staring at a disheveled blonde girl on all fours, who was blinking down at her slender fingers with evident confusion.

Aldon, who to his consternation was riding over Sir Brian's shoulder, saw the transformation happen. He stared even more than Sir Brian, his eyes growing wide as Winifred's rather large blue ones looked back up at him and warmed with recognition.

Celine had not been entirely truthful when she told Aldon that Winnie was a very beautiful girl. She was not. But she was pretty, and very sweet, and in peril, and all of this worked in Aldon a strange quickening within. Still slung over Sir Brian's shoulder, he reached for her.

She reached back.

Before their hands could meet, walls of fire burst out from the ground before and behind and cut Winifred off completely.

"Leap the wall!" Aldon shouted.

"Can't do that again, lad," Sir Brian said. Despite the fact that he was running full tilt with a dog and a shepherd over his shoulders, his voice was only slightly strained. But the strain was enough to tell Aldon that the knight was sincere.

"This whole courtyard's ablaze. We go back in, we'll never come back out."

Sir Brian ran through a door, bolted it behind him, and set his cargo down. He met Aldon's eyes with a sorrowful gaze. "The best we can do now is get out ourselves," he said. "I'm sorry."

It only took them a minute to find Tereska, who

acknowledged their presence with unspoken joy and said, "We have to save—"

"No," Sir Brian interrupted her. "We have to get out. Now."

Tereska stared at him for a moment, and then, to everyone's surprise, she nodded.

"You're right," she said. "Come with me. I know a way out."

Chapter 18

TOMAS HAULED CELINE OVER THE WINDOWSILL. She set her feet on the floor and brushed out her ivory skirts, then looked up at him with a face that was quietly beaming.

"Hello, Lady Moon," he said.

"Thank you," she answered.

He blushed and smiled back at her. Despite the fact that the world was burning down outside the window, both of them felt quietly and deeply happy.

"Do you still want to marry me?" Celine asked.

"I do," Tomas said. "But it's probably too late for that."

She looked over her shoulder at the flames outside the window. "It's the end of the world, isn't it?"

Tomas crossed to the window and looked down. The

firelight set his golden face to glowing. "Perhaps not," he said. "It's my destiny, you know, to defeat your uncle. I've come to do it."

"What can you possibly do?" Celine asked.

Tomas reached out then and took her hand. He gently led her back to the windowsill. She sat down on it. With the stone window frame, the flames behind, and her skirts falling around her, she looked like a beautiful painting.

"I am going to do my best," said Tomas. "And give what I should have given long ago."

"What is that?" Celine asked. He had moved closer, and she looked up now into his eyes. Her face still glowed in his presence—like the moon in the light of the sun.

Tomas smiled. The old, friendly, crackling home fire was in his eyes. He kissed her forehead and moved back a step. "My life," he said simply. "Look to the fountain. It's going to blow."

And then he shoved her out the window.

The plunge from the room where Tomas still stood to the stones of the courtyard was far enough to break a young woman's neck—unless someone was there to break your fall, which Winifred was. Celine landed directly on top of her, and both of them crumpled to the ground in a heap. Celine jumped up again almost as fast, grabbed Winifred's hand,

and shook her free fist at the window.

"Tomas!" she called. "You can't do this!"

Then she looked down at Winnie's pale, frightened, human face, livened by the dancing fire all around them, and smiled despite herself. "You look good," she said. "What happened?"

"I don't know," Winnie said. "Celine, we're going to die."

Celine looked past Winifred, who was struggling to her feet, down the corridor of flames to the wreckage of the spurting fountain. "No," she said. "We're not. Come on."

Half-dragging Winnie, who was unused to dealing with skirts after so many years in fur and claws and was attempting to gather hers and run—but was succeeding only in half-tripping, half-hopping along—Celine ran down the corridor of fire. She barely looked at the burning heap of the dead pyroline, nor gave in to the temptation to look for the others. Tomas's command had been direct, and she meant to follow it.

As they drew closer to the fountain, the ground began to tremble beneath their feet, as though some great power had gathered itself beneath the flagstones.

Tomas heard the ground rumbling as he stood on the windowsill and looked over the flames at the black head of the dragon and the man who sat on its neck. Wishing Celine and Winnie away and safe, he concentrated on the dragon as it spread its black wings. Quick, smooth, and nearly silent, it lifted into the air and swooped overhead. Tomas leapt from the windowsill in perfect time to catch the dragon's clawed foot and fly up with the creature.

Umbria looked down and saw Tomas struggling to climb up the dragon's foot. He cursed loudly, but somehow Tomas knew that there was no real anger in the curse. As if to confirm his impression, just as Tomas tried to move up, Umbria's hand came down and grasped his. His enemy hauled him up onto the dragon's back.

They had flown straight up over the burning castle. Tongues of the highest flames licked near their feet. The dragon's body was hot, as though a furnace burned within it. The hand Umbria offered to Tomas was red and blistered. As soon as he was seated behind the mad magician, Tomas said, "To the tower!"

How Umbria communicated with the dragon Tomas wasn't sure, but in a moment they were flying toward the north tower. Tomas and Umbria both pushed themselves up from the dragon's scaly back, and as one they jumped down together. They landed hand in hand and faced each other for a moment, each solemn as a warrior. The flames were reflected in Umbria's eyes, mingled with equal measures of mad joy and somber understanding.

"So you face me at last," Umbria said.

"Not here," Tomas said. "Can it be done?" He nodded toward the Machine.

Umbria looked at the thin rim and the controls.

"I've set it already," Tomas said. "It only needs your expertise to take us out of here."

Umbria looked back out at the burning courtyard and the dragon that still flew above them. His eyes followed the creature up into the sky, the flaming castle beneath, all of it like a terrible, glorious painting of his own creation. "It is beautiful," he muttered.

Tomas looked at him with compassion and strength. "But it cannot remain," he said. "Even you would not unleash this."

"I have unleashed it," Umbria said. Then the pride in him seemed to crumple. "But no—you are right. I can't let it remain."

The small man took himself to the controls of the Machine and began to work with them. The dragon was rising higher in the sky; the flames of the castle spreading. In a matter of minutes the fire would escape the castle and begin to burn up the landscape around it. Tomas felt the urgency inside him, beating, building, hurting. But he knew there was nothing more he could do. It all depended on Umbria now. So he turned and looked out on the courtyard, listening to the roar of the flames and the building rumble beneath the castle, and he tried to search out Celine with his eyes and wish her farewell as his heart said one last good-bye.

Tereska led them through a drab wooden door and through a series of narrow halls, all of them long-abandoned servants' passages meant to keep servants unobtrusive. The group now was anything but: Sir Brian's armour clanked as he ran, pulling a still-protesting Aldon behind him; Brig limped along, barking frequently; the crickets made a clanging racket as they jumped and landed. Tereska had Monk by the hand, and with her other hand she cleared cobwebs out of their way like a cleaning woman on a rampage.

The passage dead-ended in a wall so dusty it looked as though a sandstorm had hit it. This was, in fact, just what had happened to it, during a stage when Umbria had experimented with creating localized weather. None of the escapees knew that, though.

"Dead end!" Aldon cried. "Let's go back. We can help—"

"We *can't*," Tereska said. With her ragged arms she wiped away the layer of dust. Beneath it, a small door became visible. "This is the outside wall," she said. "It's a drop to get to the ground, but . . ."

"Stand back," Sir Brian said. He swung his battle-axe and brought it into the door. The door shattered, and pieces of wood flew in every direction. Tereska rushed forward, but Sir Brian stopped her with his arm.

"The axe rebounded," he said. "There's something else blocking the way."

Gingerly, Tereska reached out. Her fingers touched something invisible, spongy, and warm. She let out a noise that might have been a curse. "Umbria's spell," she said.

"We're trapped?" came Aldon's voice from the rear.

"We're not going back," Tereska growled. She reached inside her cloak and pulled Tomas's golden sword out once again. It had sliced through a magical seal once. It could do it again. Tereska thrust the sword straight forward. The tip went through the thick magic, half-burying the blade while the free end quivered. Tereska shoved it in farther and then tried to move the blade. It didn't want to budge. It felt as though she'd plunged it into a block of hardening molasses.

But when a woman is attempting to rescue herself, her revolution, and a big man in armour who insists on calling her "my lady" from the cruel appetites of Ravening Fire, that woman does not allow magical molasses to stand in her way. Tereska grabbed the hilt with both hands, let out a war scream that would have curdled milk, lowered her head, and charged.

The sword went the rest of the way through the magic, and Tereska went right through with it. For a moment she thought it would squeeze the life out of her. She tried to gasp, but couldn't; where air had been there was nothing now but a heavy, fuzzy pressure.

In the next moment she popped out the other side, fell six feet to the ground, and lay gasping for breath on the greensward. Through her blurry eyes she saw the others pitch themselves from the wall and land in disarray around her.

"Ouch," she heard Sir Brian mutter. "That's going to leave a dent."

Almost as one, the escaped revolutionaries and friends pushed themselves up on their elbows, turned, and looked at the blazing hulk of the palace that rose above them. Aldon's face was white. Sir Brian looked solemn.

"Oh, poor Celine," Grandfather Monk said.

In that instant an explosion sounded from within the palace walls. A column of water shot straight up in the air, bearing debris with it—including two young women. The water held them suspended over the fire for an instant, and then a blast of wind blew them beyond the walls. Tereska leaped to her feet.

"Catch them!" she shouted.

Sir Brian and Aldon were right behind her. Aldon managed to leap into position just in time to catch Winifred, who flung both arms around his neck and held on with a bewildered expression that lent itself to clinging. Celine fell half into Sir Brian's arms and half into Tereska's. She was struggling to get down almost as soon as they caught her, and they lowered her carefully. She was soaked, bedraggled, and utterly beautiful. Her eyes were on the burning castle, but she turned to the others with tears in her eyes—and then she saw the sword at Tereska's waist.

"Where did you get that?" she asked. She was nearly breathless. Tereska started to answer, but Celine didn't seem to want an answer. She held out her hands.

"Let me take it to him," she said.

Tereska met Celine's eyes. "If you go back in there . . ."

"He needs it," Celine said. "He wasn't meant to meet his destiny without it."

Tereska looked at Celine a moment longer, and then something came into her eyes that was rarely seen there. Respect.

"Or without you," she said.

She held out the sword. Celine took it with the kind of unbridled gratitude that is shown only in matters of life and death, when no one cares about maintaining dignity anymore. She turned back to the castle, then stopped one final time and turned. The raging fire behind her, licking through the stones of the castle walls now, lit her up as though she was a tongue of fire herself.

"Good-bye," she said. "Grandfather . . . Winnie. I'll always be grateful to you."

Winifred let go of Aldon's neck and slid down to her feet. Her blue eyes beseeched Celine to stay even as she held out empty hands toward her friend. Celine smiled at her. "May all go well with you," she said.

And then she turned and ran down the hill, back to the castle, sword in hand. The wooden gates gave way before the sword, and she plunged back into the inferno.

Umbria's nimble fingers worked the controls until a net had been cast over all the castle. Its white strands reached above, capturing the dragon beneath it. They crawled down the castle walls like a thing alive and plunged deep into the ground, beneath the reach of the fire that was burning down through Winnie's burrows into the dragon's cavern and further. They sealed the castle doors. The threads were fine, almost invisible, but Tomas's eyes were sharp to see magic—the eyes of a true Immortal. He saw the web spreading and knew it was just in time.

And then he saw Celine come back through the castle door, and the netting closed the doors behind her and made escape possible. He turned to shout to Umbria to stop, and in that moment Umbria pressed the final button. A burst of energy knocked Tomas off his feet and nearly sent him over the edge of the tower. He grasped the uneven stones of the floor as they began to glow. The entire palace shuddered as the bands of the web pierced through it. Tomas saw the fine strands pass through his own hands and arms and felt them as they sliced through every inch of him.

And the palace of Ignus Umbria disappeared forever from the world.

On the hillside, Tereska, Aldon, Winifred, Grandfather Monk, and the knights watched as the palace was enveloped in a golden glow and suddenly disappeared. A great black crater remained where it had been. High overhead, the guard bird circled.

The onlookers gaped at the disappearance, and then Winifred burst into tears.

Chapter 19

O N A RED, BARREN PLANET FAR AWAY, a golden glow appeared in the sky. It hovered, formed itself into a circling ball, and just as suddenly burst forth into the blazing walls and substance of a palace. It landed on the dusty surface with a faint thud. From the sky above it, a huge black dragon careened out of the air and landed, snout first, in the red dust.

When the palace appeared it was blazing, but the moment it positioned itself on the surface of the planet, several of the more adventurous tongues of flame were instantly extinguished. Fire that had been burning straight through stone and iron fell back to easier fuel or went out altogether.

Just inside the palace gates, Celine found herself standing on bare flagstones in the midst of a fire that was rapidly dying. She still held Tomas's sword in her hands. The sky above her was cloudy, the grey clouds faintly tinged with rust. Before her eyes, on the top of the shattered north tower, two men rose shakily to their feet.

"Tomas!" Celine called.

The taller of the men turned and looked down. A moment later, he flung himself off the tower, executed several flips in the air, and landed gracefully at Celine's feet.

Tomas bowed. His face was flushed, and the expression in his eyes the purest picture of absolute conflict that had ever been seen.

"Celine," he said. "I'm so glad to see you. And you should never have come. I don't how to send you home!"

Celine opened her mouth to answer him, but before she could, his eyes widened. An alarming sound, much like someone taking a deep breath before diving into dinner, came from behind Celine even as a dark shadow fell over her. Without hesitation she tossed the sword to Tomas and ducked. The dragon's jaws snapped shut just where she'd been standing. Tomas leaped forward just at the same moment and buried the sword, to the hilt, in the dragon's head. The creature hissed, lurched backwards, writhed impressively, and dissolved. All that was left of it was a black stain on the planet's surface and a golden hilt bearing the words *Umbria's Bane*.

Tomas stepped outside the palace gates with Celine close on his heels, knelt down, and picked up the bladeless hilt.

"Oh dear," he said.

"I meant you to use that to fight my uncle," Celine said.

"Oh, you did, did you?" asked another voice. Tomas and Celine whirled around as one. Tomas held out his arm, instinctively protecting Celine. Umbria was standing just behind them.

"Turned on me completely," Umbria said, glaring at Celine. He waved his hand, the gesture taking in the burning palace, the black stain that had been a dragon, and the dismal red aspect all around them. "You betrayed me to help the man who caused all *this*."

Celine opened her mouth to argue, but no word of argument came out. Instead she nodded and said, "Yes."

Tomas took her hand.

Umbria shook his head. "You're fools, both of you," he said. "What are you doing here, Celine? He got you out of the palace. You didn't have to come back."

"He needed his sword," Celine said.

"Nonsense," Umbria said. "That sword wasn't my enemy—he was. And he faced me just fine without it. Just fine indeed. Provoked my dragon and sent everything I worked for up in flames. It was a beautiful conflagration, wasn't it? It was. Beautiful. No, he didn't need that sword." Umbria pointed. "He needed you. And he's got you now. If I try to fight him like the fates would have us fight, I'll never beat him. You can't beat a man who's trying to protect his lady, especially when you've got nothing left to protect."

Tomas and Celine wore nearly identical expressions. They were confused first, and hopeful second, and rounding out the looks was a sort of piqued anxiety that indicated they wanted to argue with every other word that came out of Umbria's mouth but couldn't find words to do it fast enough.

"Wondering why it's going out?" Umbria asked. "You didn't ask, but you should have. It's going out because nothing on earth can stop Ravening Fire, and nothing beyond earth can feed it. There's nothing here for it to eat. Your martyrdom has failed, Tomas. You saved the world but didn't manage to kill yourself. That should make *you* happy, Celine. The two of you can live here together until you both grow so sick of each other you'll come crying to me for company."

Celine and Tomas looked at each other. Both were beginning to smile. They had fully intended to die for—and with—each other, but it was so much better to live together instead. The red planet around them was desperately desolate, but love can make even a dead garden bloom, and they both knew it.

So did Ignus Umbria, who had never loved anyone, but had spent far too much time studying the ways and mysteries of things not to notice that love was particularly ridiculous and particularly powerful—that it always bucked expectations and somehow succeeded despite it.

"Well," Umbria said. His fingers were in the pocket of his waistcoat, and he was fumbling about with something. He stopped them and looked piercingly at Tomas.

"Is this good enough?" he asked. "You came to face me and you sent me here. Will that do, or do you need to see me dead yet?"

"I think," Tomas said, "I think this will do."

"Well then," Umbria said, drawing something small and golden out of his pocket. "There's not much point in you staying here. You'd come crying to me, yes, you would, and I'm not sure I want either of you underfoot. Or your children!"

Celine blushed and held tighter to Tomas's hand. She leaned forward to see what Umbria was holding out to them.

It was the magic ring that had whisked Celine away from the moon and back to earth when the adventure began.

"Go on," Umbria said. "Take it."

Celine reached out and took it. The center of it still shimmered when she looked through it. The ring was small and cold, but it seemed to throb in her hand.

"You do have the other one?" Umbria asked Tomas.

"Of course," Tomas said. He reached into his pocket and drew out the other ring.

"But," Celine said, "we can't—I don't think we can fool them again."

Tomas smiled and looked down into Celine's welcoming eyes. "We don't have to, do we?" he said.

He took the ring from Celine's palm and slipped it on her finger. With a smile, he kissed her forehead. "You will marry me, Celine?"

"With all my heart," Celine answered.

Tomas put the other ring on, and as the air began to spin around them both, they heard one last shout from Ignus Umbria.

"Good riddance!"

Winifred was darning one of Aldon's stockings when a flash of light announced the return of the would-be martyrs. Celine materialized in just such a position that she nearly fell over Winnie, and as she tried to catch her balance she got tangled in the mess of yarn all about the maid, tried to catch herself on a chair, and fell in a heap instead. She sprained her ankle.

Tomas and Celine married each other the next day regardless. Celine had a bad limp, but she smiled so radiantly no one noticed—except Winnie, who was carrying her train and kept biting her lip with regret for having injured her friend for such a day.

That evening they all stood out on the hillside: Tomas and his beautiful wife, Aldon with Winifred's arm tucked in his, Tereska and Sir Brian, Grandfather Monk with tears in his now-peaceful eyes. Brig sat at their feet with the guard bird perched on his back.

"Do you see that, Lady Moon?" Tomas asked. He pointed far into the night sky where a faint red planet glowed.

"Do you suppose he'll ever come back?" Celine asked.

"He might," Tomas answered.

"If he does," Aldon cut in, "we'll all be waiting for him."

And so they were.

Rachel would love to hear from you!

CONNECT ONLINE AND GET A FREE BOOK!

Web: **www.rachelstarrthomson.com**
Facebook: **www.facebook.com/RachelStarrThomsonWriter**
Twitter: **@writerstarr**

THE ONENESS CYCLE

Exile   Hive   Attack   Renegade   Rise

The supernatural entity called the Oneness holds the world together.
What happens if it falls apart?

In a world where the Oneness exists, nothing looks the same. Dead men walk. Demons prowl the air. Old friends peel back their mundane masks and prove as supernatural as angels. But after centuries of battling demons and the corrupting powers of the world, the Oneness is under a new threat—its greatest threat. Because this time, the threat comes from within.

Fast-paced contemporary fantasy.

*"Plot twists and lots of edge-of-your-seat action,
I had a hard time putting it down!"*

—Alexis

"Finally! The kind of fiction I've been waiting for my whole life!"
—Mercy Hope, FaithTalks.com

"I sped through this short, fast-paced novel, pleased by the well-drawn characters and the surprising plot. Thomson has done a great job of portraying difficult emotional journeys . . . Read it!"

—Phyllis Wheeler, The Christian Fantasy Review

Available everywhere online or special order from your local bookstore.

THE SEVENTH WORLD TRILOGY

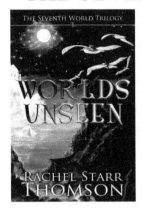  

Worlds Unseen   **Burning Light**   **Coming Day**

For five hundred years the Seventh World has been ruled by a tyrannical empire—and the mysterious Order of the Spider that hides in its shadow. History and truth are deliberately buried, the beauty and treachery of the past remembered only by wandering Gypsies, persecuted scholars, and a few unusual seekers. But the past matters, as Maggie Sheffield soon finds out. It matters because its forces will soon return and claim lordship over her world, for good or evil.

The Seventh World Trilogy is an epic fantasy, beautiful, terrifying, pointing to the realities just beyond the world we see.

"An excellent read, solidly recommended for fantasy readers."

—Midwest Book Review

"A wonderfully realistic fantasy world. Recommended."
—Jill Williamson, Christy-Award-Winning Author of ***By Darkness Hid***

"Epic, beautiful, well-written fantasy that sings of truth."

—Rael, reader

Available everywhere online or special order from your local bookstore.

TAERITH

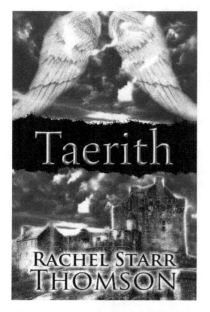

When he rescues a young woman named Lilia from bandits, Taerith Romany is caught in a web of loyalties: Lilia is the future queen of a spoiled king, and though Taerith is not allowed to love her, neither he can bring himself to leave her without a friend. Their lives soon intertwine with the fiercely proud slave girl, Mirian, whose tragic past and wild beauty make her the target of the king's unscrupulous brother.

The king's rule is only a knife's edge from slipping—and when it does, all three will be put to the ultimate test. In a land of fog and fens, unicorns and wild men, Taerith stands at the crossroads of good and evil, where men are vanquished by their own obsessions or saved by faith in higher things.

"Devastatingly beautiful . . . I am amazed at every chapter how deeply you've caused us to care for these characters."

—Gabi

"Deeply satisfying." —Kapezia

"Rachel Starr Thomson is an artist, and every chapter of Taerith is like a painting . . . beautiful."

—Brittany Simmons

Available everywhere online or special order from your local bookstore.

ANGEL IN THE WOODS

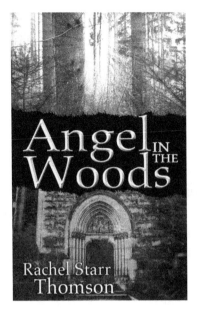

Hawk is a would-be hero in search of a giant to kill or a maiden to save. The trouble is, when he finds them, there are forty-some maidens—and they call their giant "the Angel." Before he knows what's happening, Hawk is swept into the heart of a patchwork family and all of its mysteries, carried away by their camaraderie—and falling quickly in love.

But the outside world cannot be kept at bay forever. Suspecting the Giant of hiding a treasure, the wealthy and influential Widow Brawnlyn sets out to tear the family apart and bring the Giant to destruction any way she can. And her two principle weapons are Hawk—and the truth.

Caught between the terrible truths he discovers about the family's past and the unalterable fact that he has come to love them, Hawk must face his fears and overcome his flaws if he is to rescue the Angel in the woods.

> *"A beautiful tale of finding oneself, honor and heroism; a story I will not soon forget."*
> — Szoch

> *"The more I think about it, the more truth and beauty I find in the story."*
> —H. A. Titus

Available everywhere online or special order from your local bookstore.

REAP THE WHIRLWIND

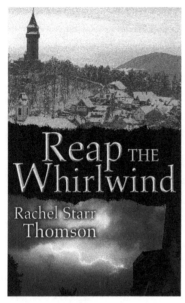

Beren is a city in constant unrest: ruled by a ruthless upper class and harried by a band of rebels who want change. Its one certainty is that the two sides do not, and will not, meet.

But children know little of sides or politics, and Anna and Kyara— a princess and a peasant girl—let their chance meeting grow into a deep friendship. Until the day Kyara's family is slaughtered by Anna's people, and the friendship comes to an abrupt end.

Years later, Kyara is a rebel—bitter, hard, and violent. Anna's efforts to fight the political system she belongs to avail little. Neither is a child anymore—but neither has ever forgotten the power of their long-ago friendship. When a secret plot brings the rebellion to a fiery head, both young women know it is too late to save the land they love.

But is it too late to save each other?

Available everywhere online.

THE PROPHET TRILOGY

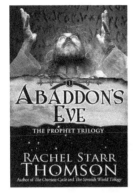

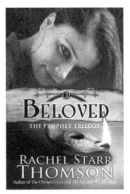

Abaddon's Eve   **Comes the Dragon**   **Beloved**

A prophet and his apprentice.
A runaway and a wealthy widow marked as an outcast.

They alone can see the terrible judgment
marching on their land.

But can they do anything to stop it?

The Prophet Trilogy is a fantasy set in
a near-historical world of deserts, temples,
and spiritual forces that vie
for the hearts of men.

Available everywhere online or special order from your local bookstore.

SHORT FICTION
BY RACHEL STARR THOMSON

Butterflies Dancing

Fallen Star

Of Men and Bones

Ogres Is

Journey

Magdalene

The City Came Creeping

Wayfarer's Dream

War With the Muse

Shields of the Earth

And more!

Available as downloads for
Kindle, Kobo, Nook, iPad, and more!

CPSIA information can be obtained
at www.ICGtesting.com
Printed in the USA
JSHW051213190222
22905JS00012B/31

9 781927 658413